J. Arpitt

CW00972995

GUS THE HUMAN GOOSE

Dear Ieuan,

I hope you enjoy

my first novel!

from Julie Arpitt

xxy

GUS THE HUMAN GOOSE

JULIE CUPITT

The Book Guild Ltd

First published in Great Britain in 2023 by
The Book Guild Ltd
Unit E2 Airfield Business Park,
Harrison Road, Market Harborough,
Leicestershire. LE16 7UL
Tel: 0116 2792299
www.bookguild.co.uk
Email: info@bookguild.co.uk
Twitter: @bookguild

Typeset in 12pt Minion Pro

Printed on FSC accredited paper
Printed and bound in Great Britain by 4edge Limited

ISBN 978 1915603 777

British Library Cataloguing in Publication Data.
A catalogue record for this book is available from the British Library.

FOR CLARA AND ALEXANDER,
WITH ALL MY LOVE

That You Probably Didn't Know...

6) There are 8 goose years in every human year. Basically, if you and a goose are born on the same day, when you're a cute two-year-old human, the goose will be a stroppy teenager

7) Geese are better at fighting off burglars than dogs

8) There are 30 species of goose in the whole world

9) A goose's favourite food is blueberries. Except for Gus, the star of this story. His is chocolate cake

10) Sometimes a goose is fed up of being a goose. He'd rather be just like us...

Except the ones i completely made up...

PROLOGUE

MY MUMMY!

Did you know, that when you first arrive in the world from your mum's tummy, the first thing you see is what you think you are?

Once there was a boy raised in the forest by wolves – he thought he was a wolf and liked howling at the moon! Or you might have heard about the baby girl, who was accidentally handed to a Siberian tiger by a silly nurse. She grew up with a taste for raw meat and enjoyed hunting little children to eat. Okay – so I made the last one up, because you don't usually see tigers walking around hospitals. But this sort of thing *can* happen!

Well, this is a story about a wild goose, who this kind of thing ACTUALLY happened to. The goose would later be named Gus, but we don't know that yet, because the story is only just beginning, and Gus hasn't hatched from his egg yet.

Anyway, one windy but sunny day, a proud mummy-goose-to-be called Goosabella was guarding her egg high up on a tree branch. When WHOOSH! A large gust of wind knocked the egg onto the floor, where it rolled down the steep hill and into a nearby children's playground. That day, two nice, well-behaved, eight-year-old children (a lot like you) were playing after school. Those children were called Clara and Boris and were little geeks who listened properly in their lessons (maybe not like you then!).

'Boris, Boris!' shrieked Clara. 'It's that goose egg we've been watching the mummy goose in the tree guard every day! It must've rolled out! Help – we MUST get it back to the goose mummy, and QUICK! If it hatches in my hands the baby goose will think it's human if I'm the first thing it sees! Miss taught us about this in biology, remember?'

'It's a mission, Clara,' shrieked Boris, as he hastily pulled his favourite Batman cape from his school bag and fastened it around his neck. They both ran as fast as their legs would carry them up the hill.

'Nearly there,' cried Clara, puffing and panting, her blonde pigtails swishing back and forth as she ran through the wind.

'Over there Clara, I can see a *load* of geese flapping and honking, it must be the family! They must be *super* worried, quick, QUICK!'

The family of geese swooped all around Clara

and Boris, honking with excitement as they realised what the children were bringing to them.

But it was *too* late…

Just as Clara got ready to hand the egg back to its mummy, a sharp beak poked out, revealing fluffy feathers as the rest of the egg shattered around it.

The tiny, new-born goose looked up at Clara with loving eyes and honked its very first words: 'MY MUMMY!'

ONE

SIXTEEN GOOSE YEARS (TWO HUMAN YEARS) LATER

'Gus, Gus – come on, get in, will you! Stop standing on that riverbank like a wuss with your feathers all clean! Get in this glorious mud! Ooh... I love the way it clings to my white feathers and makes them all mucky and brown! So sticky, so sloshy. Rub it all over you! Mm, mm, mmmmm. Get IN!'

Gus shot his best friend Cuthbert a look of disgust. He *hated* mud. Cuthbert might love wallowing in it like a pig, but Cuthbert was a silly old goose. Gus liked to have his own space. Just him and his daydreams. No Cuthbert, no parents... certainly no mud.

'Anyway, my boy... what are you up to tonight? I fancy a nice energetic swim... need to burn off some energy and keep my wing muscles in top shape. Then I'm meeting some of the girls to watch those new blades of grass along the river grow. Thomasina's coming, you know,' Cuthbert continued, raising his eyebrow feathers and giving Gus a cheeky wink. 'I think she *fancies* you…'

Tuning out Cuthbert's enthusiastic hissing, Gus shuddered with horror at the thought of his other friend, Thomasina, fancying him. He gazed across the water, looking for better stuff to think about. To the right, there was a brightly lit disco boat chugging under Putney Bridge. *Humans dancing!* All he got to do was watch grass grow and bathe in mud!

On the other bank, fancy restaurants glowed as they served up tasty meals. *Humans eating!* He'd peered through their windows before and seen delicious-looking cupcakes with icing piled high. All geese got to eat was dead, brown grass!

Tonight, he would *not* hang out with Cuthbert and the gang to watch grass grow. He would fly around the riverside restaurants, eavesdropping on human conversations and eating their leftover cake crumbs.

Humans… watching them was his favourite hobby. Ever since he'd hatched in the hands of one, he felt more like them than other geese, and liked to watch them to feel close to them. *They* got to live in beautiful houses and shower in warm water. *He* had to sleep in a mucky river. *They* went to exciting parties and talked about films and video games. *He* had to yawn through dull, goosey conversation.

Gus shook his glossy, black feathers, spraying droplets of water like a dog fresh from a bath. If he could shake all goosey stuff away from him, he would. As far as he could see, *everything* humans got was better. They even had interesting jobs where they earned money to spend on great things, like a trip to McDonald's or a skiing holiday. Hard work got a goose none of this stuff. He stared beady-eyed as the realisation hit him smack-bang on his beak. He would NEVER be satisfied as a boring bunch of hissing feathers, standing on the sidelines watching human life go by. He wanted to BE human himself. Now if only he could find a way…

*

'Gus, Gus,' honked his mum, Goosabella, swooping towards him, ruining his lovely thoughts. 'Is that YOU over there, my darling? I was thinking we could have a nice, little chat about your ideas for the Prime Goose election.'

Oh no, not that AGAIN! It was all Mum jabbered on about these days. He hastily searched for an escape route, but it was too late: she'd seen him! She'd corner him with her sharp beak and never let him go.

'Now that you're growing up, you really need to think about making something of yourself. You know, your dad's been the flock's best EVER Prime

Goose, it would make us *so* proud if our precious son could keep the title in the family!'

Blah, blah, blah, blah, blah. Gus began zoning out as she continued honking in his face.

'In fact, just this afternoon, I overheard Cuthbert telling Thomasina about his life's ambition to become the next Prime Goose!' Mum whacked him on the head to make sure he was listening properly. 'If you're not careful, he'll snatch the honour from right under your beak...'

'Oh, come off it, Mum, you're making it up!' Out of the corner of his eye, he saw Cuthbert in the distance, licking bits of mud off the ground and squealing with delight. 'He's an idiot. He's a silly mummy's boy who can't even forage for his own breakfast!'

'Well, at least he has ambition! YOU need to get some ambition, a work ethic, a *dream*...' she honked back defiantly, getting so close her beak almost poked his eye out.

'I do have dreams,' Gus hissed quietly, looking down at the ground. 'Just not the same ones you and Dad have for me.'

'So then, *Gus*, what great ideas *do you* have for your campaign to be elected as the next Prime Goose? I can imagine a smart, mature gander like yourself has given this some serious thought. I am VERY much looking forward to hearing them!'

'Oh, Mum, is THAT the time?' Gus screeched

4

with mock hysteria. 'I told Grandad I would be at his for dinner at seven, remember?'

With that parting comment he flew off at top speed before Mum could stop him, scattering a few feathers as he went. Once out of her sight, he splashed into the river to wash the remaining mud off his legs. He couldn't turn up at Grandad's house dirty! Mud was definitely not his thing.

TWO

DINNER WITH GRANDAD

Dinner with Grandad was Gus's favourite part of the week. If he'd wanted to grow old as a goose – which he certainly didn't – Grandad was exactly the type of gander he'd want to be. He was a large and imposing but wrinkly old bird, who commanded respect wherever he flew. Grandad also had a cool nickname – 'OG'. This stood for 'Old Goose', but for a laugh Gus told Cuthbert it stood for 'Original Gangster'. Once he'd stuck his beak into the window of a riverside flat and seen two men watching a programme on television about 'gangsters' – so Gus knew *all* about them!

'How's my favourite grandson then?' Gus felt his grandad's gentle wing playfully cuff him around the head as they greeted each other. 'It's nice to see you early for once, you're usually late for everything. I wasn't expecting to see you for at least another two hours!'

'Don't be stupid, Grandad, I'm your only grandson!'

'I know, I know, but you're my favourite anyway.' Grandad smiled and gave him a slobbery kiss on the cheek with his beak.

'Arghhh, gross, cut it out, Grandad! I'm not a gosling anymore.'

'Okay, okay, I'll stop.' Grandad fixed him with a cheeky grin. 'If you promise to tell me why you're so early!'

'I, er… er… thought I'd arrive early to help you forage for dinner.'

'Stop lying, Gus, I didn't hatch yesterday! I don't suppose it's something to do with escaping your mother's little chat about the Prime Goose election? I flew into her this afternoon. She said she wanted to talk to you about your ideas.'

'Oh, that flippin' Prime Goose thing AGAIN! Gimme a break! Everyone wants to have a go at me these days. Life's so not fair.'

'Take that sulky look off your eyes and beak and sit up properly. It's disrespectful to slouch around your elders!'

'Sorry, Grandad, I've just had a *dreadful* week. Mum's done nothing but nag and, like, earlier this week, Cuthbert spread a rumour around the gang that Thomasina fancies me. I go bright red when she starts showing off or stroking her head feathers with her wing. It's *soooo* embarrassing!'

Grandad stifled a laugh. 'Oh, it's *so hard* growing up, isn't it? All the weight of the world on your wings! Try not to be too hard on your mum, though, she just wants the best for you.'

'Okay, okay,' Gus groaned, with his flight feathers crossed behind his back. 'I promise to be nicer to Mum.'

'That's my grandson! Anyway, cheer up, I have a treat for you this evening.'

'Really?' Gus's feathers tingled in anticipation.

Could this be the night when Grandad would at last tell him his life story – of how he lived amongst humans and met Granny Goosietta? Before he and Granny emigrated to the flocks of South West London to raise Mum. Gus had heard snippets of information from Mum about how Grandad grew up on a farm, but he was desperate to hear the whole tale. He'd been begging Grandad to tell him for *years*.

Grandad smiled, his shrewd black eyes sparkling. 'You're old enough now, Gus. I think it's finally time I told you the story of how I became a Guard Goose, and how you came to be born.'

THREE

Cherry Blossom Farm

'Two generations of geese ago, back when I was young, I was playing *flying races* with my gaggle. Ah, I was such a strong, competitive creature, not the wrinkly old goose you see today.' Grandad smiled. 'Anyway, this one day began like every other: breakfast… races before lunch. But then *everything* changed! I was full of bravado, trying to prove I was the fastest, best gander of the gang, hurtling so fast I couldn't stop, headed towards a window… Well, that was the last thing I remember. I must've hit the glass, because when I awoke, I was lying on the riverbank, feeling lightheaded, with stars in front of my eyes!'

'*Ah*, so that's why you're so forgetful! I thought it was just because you're ancient.'

'Do you want to hear this story or not, Gus? You've been asking me about it for years. Then, when I start telling it, you butt in with your cheeky beak before I've even finished the second sentence. Seriously, your mum might have a point when she says you need to grow up a bit.'

Gus looked at his webbed feet. 'Sorry, Grandad, I'm only messing. But can you get to the bit about the humans? What are they like? Are their lives really as wonderful as they look? I don't know anyone who can tell me about them, except you.'

'All in good time, Gus. You young ganders are so impatient. Be quiet and listen.'

Gus fiddled with his feathers and put on his best 'thoughtful listening face'.

'Anyway, as I was saying, before I was rudely interrupted… when I came round, this lovely human lady was cuddling me and stroking my feathers. Her name was Sarah Greyson and I loved her like she was my own mother. She took me home to her parents' place, a lovely farm called Cherry Blossom, and nursed me back to health.'

Gus puffed up his feathers and scowled, failing to hide his jealousy. He wished *he* had an interesting human mum. His own mum didn't understand him and was literally the most uncool goose ever. All she ever did was nag.

'What was Sarah like, Grandad? And the farm? Did you have *human* friends? Did you get to hang out with them and eat human food and do human things? Come on, tell me, tell me, TELL ME!'

'Oh, Gus, I was so lucky to be found by her. She

really was the kindest, sweetest human – and so clever too. Just before I emigrated here, she went off to study zoology at Oxford University. She couldn't understand my honks and hisses, but we chatted all the time! She even told me that her ambition was to design a video game where players could experience being a goose – because geese are so awesome!

'Oh, and I loved her parents too! Her mum Bettina was the best cook ever, I can still remember the taste of her gooey, chocolate fudge cake… and her dad, Abel, well, he was an egg farmer. He kept domestic Chinese geese to lay them – but more on that later!'

'University?' Gus asked, picking up on the bit that sounded most interesting. 'What's that?! Geese don't have *university*! If humans get to go, I want to go too!'

'Oh, it's a place humans go to when they're slightly older than you, actually. They choose a subject that interests them, work hard at it and then spend their evenings going to parties. Sarah had an older sister called Cressie, who was at university too. Once I overheard her tell Sarah down the phone about how her and her friends drank loads of beer, had a crazy riverside party, then dived into the River Thames for a swim! No doubt they landed on the heads of some poor, unsuspecting Canada geese!'

Gus snorted in annoyance. Typical. Parties – something else fun humans got to do that geese didn't. 'Um, hang on, Grandad… you've told me about the humans, but what did *you* actually do all day around them? Did you get to go to university too?'

Grandad let out a belly-roaring snort of laughter. 'Oh, no, Gus,' he said, 'a goose would look ridiculous in a graduation gown and cap. You know humans and geese have very different lives.'

Gus looked down at the floor. He knew that far too well.

'No, I became what humans call a *house pet*. That means I was pampered and looked after by the humans, unlike the working farm animals. It was great at first. They fed me amazing food, let me watch exciting TV programmes and even take part in board games. There was this one I was great at, called Monopoly. Most humans just don't realise how intelligent we geese are. They thought I was shredding the fake money with my beak, but actually I was trying to buy a house in Mayfair!'

'But why was it only great at first, Grandad?'

'Well, I didn't want to be a goose of leisure. I wanted something useful to do. Like those domestic geese who laid eggs for Abel to sell. Or the farm guard dog, a slobbery, greedy old chap called Scrapper. He had the most important job of all – protecting the farm from criminals! Oh, and I did love chatting to the other farmyard animals. One Chinese goose really stood out. She was so smart and beautiful, we had the most *romantic* dates flying around the farm, you know, hissing and honking *all* through the night. I fell head over webbed feet in love with her.'

'Granny Goosietta?' asked Gus. He'd heard stories about the great Granny Goosietta from other flock members before. Sadly he never met her – she had died from a bad bout of goose flu just before he was born.

'Yes, Granny Goosietta, she was a fine old bird, you'd have loved her, Gus. She was so interesting to hiss and honk with.'

Gus gave his second snort of annoyance that evening. Again, typical. There were only three interesting geese ever to fly the planet apparently – his grandad, Granny Goosietta and, of course, himself.

And one of them he never even got to meet!

'Hang on, but Grandad, you said Scrapper the dog was the farm guard. I thought it was you?'

'Oh, it was, it was,' said Grandad, with a casual wave of his wing. 'I'm just getting to *that* part of the story…'

FOUR

A DIAMOND RING

'Now, remember I told you Sarah had an older sister called Cressie? Well, one summer, she dropped out of university and moved back home, so that her poor parents could do *all* her cooking and laundry – even though she was an adult human! She was *not* my sort of human at all – very lazy indeed! *McFly, yah, would you be a good goosey and fetch me my magazine*, I'd hear her yell in her loud, bossy voice!'

'*McFly?* So THAT'S your real name.' Gus honked so loud with laughter he fell to the floor. 'What a stupid name for a bird.' Now he was rolling around hysterically, thumping his webbed feet in joy.

'Alright, enough, cheeky so-and-so,' said Grandad, cuffing Gus around the beak. 'It was actually the name Sarah gave to me, after a boy band she liked. I saw them on TV once and wasn't a fan of their silly haircuts and baggy jeans. But no, it wasn't my real name. My biological goose mother would've chosen a name beginning with the sound 'goos' like all other geese in my generation. I can't remember that name now, though, I lost most of my early memories after falling from that window.'

Gus smiled. He sure was glad it had gone out of fashion to give geese stupid names beginning with the sound 'goos'.

'Grandad, you said you'd tell me how you became a Guard Goose. What's this silly Cressie got to do with that?'

'Well, when she moved back home, she announced that she was engaged to be married. She even brought her fiancé back to live at the farm. Bettina was *not* impressed. And to make matters worse, her husband-to-be, a chap named Henry Inigo Boniface Wellington-Smythe III, was a wet wuss of a human. When we first met, I flapped my wings in excitement, hissing and honking, ready to chest-bump him. I just wanted to say hello. But the silly man ran away crying. I heard Bettina tell Abel that Cressie was only marrying him because he gave her this huge, sparkly engagement ring.'

'It's so not fair, Grandad. Why don't geese have cool rings with shiny stones?' Gus said petulantly.

'There are loads of cool things about being a goose, Gus. We couldn't wear rings, though, they'd just slip off our feathers. And when I tell you the *next* part of the story, you'll be glad we don't have them...'

Gus respected his grandad very much, but he had to disagree with him on there being 'loads of cool things about being a goose'. Geese were, like, basically, the most *snoresome* thing ever.

'But before I tell you the last part of the story, come on, Gus, let's eat! Your mum won't be happy if I send her pride and joy home hungry! Come over here, I spent all day preparing this.'

Grandad placed his wing on Gus's back and the two ganders waddled a little further up the riverbank. 'Sit, Gus, dinner's ready!'

Gus heard some rustling, then Grandad laid something out in front of him. 'Seaweed, freshly picked this afternoon downstream, from the estuary.' He beamed proudly. 'With a side of fresh grasses and clover. Healthy food for a growing gander – enjoy!'

Grandad had clearly gone to a lot of effort – this wasn't the usual, on-the-go, fast-food insect dinner that Gus grabbed with his parents before Dad flew off to his important meetings about Prime Goosey stuff. He took a bite. It was crunchy, a bit salty and it would be delicious… if he had wanted to be a goose and eat goose things. He turned his head away from Grandad to hide his disappointment. Grandad was cooler than this, surely – why hadn't he foraged some human food as a special treat for this special evening? Gus wanted burger, fries and milkshake – not seaweed!

FIVE

GUARD GOOSE

'Are you ready to hear how your old grandad became a Guard Goose then?'

'Mffwurfufff', grunted Gus, spraying bits of salty seaweed and clover in his grandad's direction. A few sticky bits clung naughtily to the edges of his beak. Dinner was a disappointment, but he was starving so stuffed glob after glob into his beak before swallowing the previous mouthful.

'Once upon a time... it was a dark, dark night at Cherry Blossom Farm, and all residents, human and animal, except Scrapper the guard dog, were fast asleep. Two human thieves with something very sparkly in mind – Cressie's engagement ring – entered the premises.'

Gus fidgeted with anticipation.

'Now, you remember before, I told you Scrapper was a greedy fellow who thought with his stomach first? Like most dogs.'

'Yes, Grandad.'

'Well, one of the thieves made sausages, cooked them and then mashed up some sleeping pills to hide inside them. You see, he had it all planned out. I later heard he knew all about the ring because Cressie was blabbing about it in her big showy-off voice, when out and about at London parties.'

'What a stupid human,' Gus said rather rudely. 'I thought humans were meant to be clever.'

'No, Gus, humans are just like geese and every other animal in that way. Some are very clever, a few are very stupid and there are lots of types in between.'

Gus snorted with laughter. He knew more than *a few* stupid geese, and Cuthbert definitely topped the list.

'So, you can probably guess what happened next... as soon as Scrapper smelt the sausages, he was a goner. He chomped them down, forgetting it was his job to bark and alert the household. Then with a stomach fat and full of sausage, he fell fast asleep...

'The two thieves then used a crowbar to lever open the window in the farmhouse kitchen, where I was fast asleep in my goose bed – a lovely little basket plumped with pretty pillows made by Bettina. The noise woke me up. I instantly *knew* something was wrong, so I poked my beak out of my pillows. What a sight met my eyes! Two strange-looking men, one very big and one very skinny, were creeping through the kitchen. They hadn't seen me. What a surprise I gave them! I looked squarely at those thieves and honked as if my life depended on it...

'*HONKKKKKKKKK HONKKKKKKKKK HONKKKKKKKKK HONKKKKKKKKK*, I went, before flying at them at top speed. I was ready for a battle, I can tell you! The looks on their faces! The one thing they were *not* expecting to see was a goose in the kitchen! Their mouths dropped open. But they didn't stick around. They clambered back out the window and were away, running as fast as they could towards their car. But not before I left my mark on them. I bit a few chunks out of their trousers and bottoms. The skinny thief was much harder to bite as he was rather bony, but the big one was pretty chubby and juicy!'

'Wow, Grandad, I can't believe you had a fight with real human thieves! I want to do something as cool as this!'

'Obviously Abel, Bettina and the girls heard all the commotion and came running down from their bedrooms. I nodded my beak in the direction of a piece of curled-up paper which I had seen lying on the floor. It said:

Plan to steel Big fat
ring from farmers dorter
By spike Baycon

1. Travel to cherree Blosum farm

2. distract hairee sloBurry gard dog

3. Open farmhouse Kitchen windo with crowBar

4. Find farmers dorters Bedroom

Farmers
Dorters
Bedroom

5. Chop ofs her ring finga

6. Escape thru Kitchen windo

21

'Everyone stared at the note. One of the thieves was extremely stupid and had written the plan with his name on a piece of paper!'

'Wow, Grandad, you're a hero.'

'I was pretty proud if I do say so myself. Abel swooped me up in his arms, stroked my feathers and said, "You, McFly, are a truly amazing goose. From now on, Cherry Blossom Farm is not a farm with a guard dog, but a farm with a guard goose." And that, my favourite grandson, is the story of how I became Guard Goose.'

SIX

THE MISSION

A-sniff, a-hiss, a-sniff, plop, plop, plop.

'Gus – what *on earth* is wrong?' Grandad asked, looking horrified, as big fat tears rolled down his feathers and onto the floor. 'I don't get it – one minute you're happily enjoying my story, the next minute you're a snivelling ball of feathery sadness! Didn't you like my story? Come on, tell me. Was the bit about the burglars too scary?'

'Oh, don't be so stupid, Grandad,' Gus hissed through snotty snivels. 'What kind of a wimp do you think I am?'

'Come on then, honk it out, tell me what the problem is.'

'I… I… I… I just don't want to be a goose anymore,' Gus blurted out. 'I was never *meant* to be a goose. I HATE them. Hissy, mucky, feathered things that swim in dirty water and do dull stuff

23

like watching grass *grow*. Your story is just another reminder of how much fun there is in the world outside of being a *goose*.' He stamped his webbed foot in annoyance, kicking up a load of dried-up bits of mud.

'What the heavens are you talking about, Gus? Not meant to be a goose? Don't be so ridiculous. A goose is what you are. You've got feathers, right?! A beak. You fly. Live by the river. See, if it isn't a goose that I see in front of me, I don't know what the heavens you are or would want to be, Grandson!'

'HUMAN.'

'Oh.' Grandad went quiet. With a worried look, he gently placed his wing on Gus's. 'Tell me, where have these feelings come from?'

'Well… when I was little, Mum told me the story about how I hatched in the human girl's hands. You know, I never felt quite right in my own feathers, and always wanted to find out more about life beyond our boring old goose world…

'So, I started off stalking humans, circling around their heads as they dined outside eating pizza at riverside restaurants. My friends thought I was dead weird! But I loved what I saw… the food they ate, the games they played, the comfy houses they lived in! It all made complete sense! Then earlier today… BAM! The realisation hit me hard. I will NEVER be satisfied being an awful old goose. I have to be human! I just *have* to!

'And now your story has filled me with even more excitement than I thought possible. It must happen now! I cannot waste one more day of my precious life being a goose. Human world: WATCH OUT! Here I come…'

'Oh, Gus, Gus, Gus!' sighed Grandad. 'If I'm entirely honest, I've had a dreadful worry about this at the back of my mind ever since you hatched in the hands of that little human girl. I hoped you'd forget over time and enjoy all the awesome things there are to the life of a goose. But that hasn't happened, has it?'

'No. If anything, I feel more and more out of place as I grow up. I just don't belong here. My friends all bore the feathers off me with their stupid, boring conversations about mud and grass, and I'm sick of Mum and Dad nagging me about ridiculous rubbish like this Prime Goose election. I don't want to be a bloomin' goose, let alone the leader of a whole flock of them! I want legs and arms! I want feet! And hands! I want to wear clothes! I want to go to this *university* place and play video games and go to parties! I want to eat cake and drink wine until I puke! And watch TV! And hang out with fun human friends! I bet humans don't get nagged about being a Prime Goose all the time by their silly mothers. I want to find a way to become human… I *need* to find a way to become human. It's all I think about and the only way I'll EVER be happy,' Gus concluded dramatically.

'Well, Gus, one thing you must remember, though, is that the grass isn't always greener. Yes, the human world can be very exciting, but it isn't without its problems. You know, when your mother hatched, it caused a bit of a rumpus. Abel knew instantly she was a mixed-breed gosling. I mean, that man knows geese. You see, humans aren't meant to mix different breeds of goose. That's because if they want to sell the geese in future, the purebred ones are most valuable.'

'So, because you had a baby together, Abel knew you and Granny Goosietta were married?'

'Oh yes,' said Grandad. 'We were worried the humans would find a way to keep me away from my wife and newly hatched daughter. The human world has rules and certain ways of doing things – it's not like having the freedom that you get being a wild goose! So, to protect my family from being split up, I decided we must escape. In the middle of the night, Goosietta, baby Goosabella and I snuck out quietly and flew towards London, where we settled on these banks of the River Thames.'

Gus burst into a fresh load of tears, his shoulders heaving up and down dramatically.

'What now, Gus?' Grandad sighed.

'You mean to say that even boring, uncool *Mum* got to live amongst humans once! She wouldn't even appreciate it! And here I am, a fun, adventurous goose stuck in the wild with only a load of boring, feathered creatures!'

26

'Look, you're being rather rude now. Your mum loves you and would do anything for you, so stop being so mean about us geese that happen to be your family! However, if you are deadly serious about wanting to become human, I have a friend from my days at the farm who *might* be able to help. If anyone knows how to transform someone into a different species, it's him. He's called Siegfried F. Goosman – I could get in touch and arrange a meeting…

'BUT, and I mean it, there's a big BUT… you must prove to me that you are certain this is what you want before I let you meet Mr Goosman. He's an important man and I don't want to waste his time. I know you. You get a bit carried away without thinking things through. There are serious consequences. You'd miss your mother; you couldn't exactly live in your river house with your goose parents if you were human, now, could you? And you'd have to go to something called 'school' and work hard. That's something humans your age do. It's not all fun and games, you know!'

'Yeah, yeah,' said Gus, dismissively waving his wing. 'Just tell me how on earth I can prove it so I can meet Mr Goosman and he can get on with making me human!'

'Right, Gus. I'm setting you a mission. It's called MISSION: HUMAN. Your first task is to find out as much as you can about humans and report back to me with your findings. I want to be sure that you truly understand what it means to become one. The good and the bad…'

SEVEN

THE BAD BACON BROTHERS

'*SHUT* THOSE HONKING GOBS... OR I'M COMING *RIGHT* DOWN TO TWIST YOUR NECKS OFF AND MINCE YOU INTO SAUSAGE MEAT...'

Eurgh. Those ghastly riverside geese beneath his flat window almost made Bruce Bacon abandon his favourite dinner and run to the toilet to puke up lumpy-sausage sick. Turning his attention away from the cretinous creatures he continued stuffing his face. Grease from the twenty sausages – stacked like a Jenga tower on his plate – dripped all the way into his lap, down his trousers and then plopped onto the floor. There, it lay in slimy, congealed pools.

'Sausage?' he grunted at his long, ghoulishly thin brother, who was appropriately named Spike.

'Nah, Bruv,' replied Spike. 'I'll just stick with me one piece of bread.'

'I can barely think straight,' Bruce growled. 'Those revolting good-for-nothing geese honking under the window are ruining my concentration.' He peered out of the window again and shook his fist menacingly at them. 'I SAID SHUT IT, YOU FOUL-BEAKED FEATHER DUSTERS!'

'We don't 'ave a good track record with them bloomin' gooses, do we, Bruv?' Spike replied, giving his best goofy smile to try and cheer Bruce up.

'When there is more than one goose, you say GEESE, idiot!'

'All right, Bruv, whoa, take a chill pill!' retorted Spike. 'All right, GEESE it is. So, anyway, as I was sayin', we don't 'ave much luck when it comes to gooses, do we?'

Bruce sighed in exasperation. It went in one ear and out of the other with Spike. He also hated it when his brother reminded him of that disaster a few years earlier – when they got outwitted by, of all creatures, a pet goose on a farm! He shuddered as he recalled the five years he spent in prison because of that blasted goose. And how he was still the butt of all jokes in the gangster underworld.

'Yeah, don't remind me, numbskull! If you hadn't written the plan with your name on a piece of paper like the idiot you are, we might've got away with it. Prison was awful. The food was so disgusting

I practically wasted away to nothing. I went in weighing twenty-five stone, and left weighing just twenty-two stone, nothing but skin and bone!'

'Oh, flippin' heck!' Bruce grumbled, suddenly remembering something. His day was going from bad to worse.

'What now, Bruv?'

'That lemon-sucking witch Doris is dropping my Boris off tomorrow morning to spend the day with me,' Bruce grumbled, his face dark like a thunderstorm. 'The only thing she's good for is the money she gives me to raise Boris.' He hated his ex-wife nearly as much as he hated *that goose*. She divorced him when he got sent to prison, because she was too embarrassed to stay married to a man stupider than a wild goose. He recoiled with shame as he remembered a newspaper headline at the time – '*SILLIER THAN A SILLY OLD GOOSE*' – with a very unflattering photo of his chubby mug underneath it.

'Oh, Bruv, he ain't so bad, your Boris. I don't have much in common with him, mind, he's always talking about them clever fings he learns in school, but he's a nice boy.'

'I can't believe such an embarrassment of a boy is my own son,' said Bruce. 'He's such a wuss with his nose constantly in a book. Anyway, soon I will be lying on a tropical beach, rolling in the cash, gorgeous girlfriend by my side, away from all of this rubbish.'

''Ow's that gonna 'appen, Bruv? You ain't got no money! None of 'em scary gangsters want to work with you after that goose on Cherry Blossom Farm made you look so silly!'

Resisting the urge to crush Spike, Bruce instead crushed his finished can of beer and threw it out of the window. He watched with satisfaction as it drifted down the River Thames.

'Because, IDIOT, I have *big* plans. We're going to pull off a successful jewellery heist to make me as rich as I *finally* deserve. And this time… THERE WON'T BE A GHASTLY GOOSE IN SIGHT!'

EIGHT

What Humans Do

Whistling to himself, Gus flew in the direction of Grandad's river patch, closer to the clusters of human homes. Today was Day One of his important mission. Years of sticking his nosy beak into flat windows had taught him lots about humans, but he needed to *prove* how much of an expert he was to Grandad by writing it all down. Otherwise Grandad would never introduce him to this mysterious Mr Goosman, and he'd be stuck being an *awful* goose for the rest of his life.

'GET IN HERE, SON.'

Feathers quivering, Gus bent his knees to shrink his body as small as possible. Instinctively, the tips of his wings flew up to cover his face. He recognised THAT voice instantly – last night it had threatened to mince him and Grandad into sausage meat! Grandad was getting a bit deaf with old age, so luckily he hadn't heard.

Cautiously, he lowered each wing one at a time,

checking with his beady eyes that Grandad wasn't around that morning to witness him being a wimp.

Phew! Grandad was nowhere to be seen. Instead, he saw a small, chubby boy human with a kind face. It sat on a riverside bench, holding what looked like a few pieces of paper bound together.

Tentatively, Gus waddled a few steps closer to get a better look. He peered at the human, beak square on.

'Argh, wild goose,' the boy squeaked, jumping up and dropping his pen and papers, before scuttling towards the block of flats.

Flying up to the bench, Gus swiped the papers – discreetly, he hoped – and flew up to a suitable vantage point with it. Enjoying the sun gently warming his feathers, he flicked through the pages of his new possession with his beak. 'CLASS NOTEBOOK – BORIS BACON,' Gus read aloud from the front page.

Year 6 English Assignment: Write about a member of your family

My dad, by Boris Bacon, age 10
    I love my dad very much because he is my father, but we are very different people. I am very determined not to grow up like him!
    Dad is very smart, but he did no work at school. This is a shame because

my dad is clever and could have been anything that he wanted to be (I got that line from a song in the musical Bugsy Malone!). Sadly, he chose to be a thief and was sent to prison for trying to steal a diamond ring. Now I know that if you want to achieve something in life, you have to work hard at something which does not involve naughty stuff, like stealing, which could get you locked up! Prison doesn't sound like fun!! Dad said the food was rubbish. He likes his food a lot, like me. This is the only thing we have in common.

When I grow up I want to be a lawyer, not a thief like my dad. This is because I like reading lots of things and I am also in the school debating team. My team always wins! I know I will make a good lawyer because Mum says I am an argumentative little pain. I have heard that being good at arguing makes you a great lawyer!

Dad does not understand why I like reading. He says I am a silly wimp of a boy and I should do normal things like playing video games, farting and watching football...

Ah, so this is what a 'NOTEBOOK' was for. Something humans used to write their important thoughts in. Making himself comfortable, Gus poised the pen in his beak and began making notes on what he knew about humans so far, using his best beak-writing to impress Grandad.

What do humans eat?

AMAZING things like apple crumble and cake. Like what Bettina at Cherry Blossom Farm made. MUCH more exciting than the corn and dead grass by the river that geese eat!!!

Note to self: find out if humans do actually eat goose sausages like that nasty bully, or if he was just trying to scare me. If they do, this could cause a problem...

How do humans spend their days?

Some humans go to university and spend their evenings partying, like Cressie. Unlike geese. All we do is fly, forage and swim. SNORE SNORE SNORE.

Note to self: need to find out about other things that humans can do, like being a lawyer (whatever that is!) and arguing all day as I learnt from Boris's essay. I'd be good at that.

How do humans travel?

In things that Grandad calls 'cars', which do all the hard work for them. I see too many of them moving across Putney Bridge. They also have planes. They actually get INTO something with wings to fly for them! Again so much better than being a goose, we have to use our own feathered wings to do ALL the hard work for us — SO NOT FAIR.

Where do humans live?

In things called houses and flats. These look rather cosy — I have stuck my nosy beak into a few open windows whilst spying on humans in the past! They have much more comfortable bedding to sleep in.

Geese have to sleep outside in the water to stop predators eating us! The best thing about human houses is they are MUCH more secure from predators than sleeping in a river or lake. Of course, humans can be at the mercy of predators sometimes, though, when they are not lucky enough to have a Guard Goose like my grandad!

What do humans wear?

Colourful things called 'clothes'. These all look very pretty and exciting. Geese just walk around with our feathers on our backs! I see lots of humans wearing smart things as they walk into the tube train stations every morning — Grandad said these are called suits. They are SUPER stylish — my feathered midsection would look dashingly good in one!

Note to self: investigate where to buy a suit that will fit a goose. I plan on dressing like a human whilst I figure out how to become a REAL one — then I can fit into human-shaped clothes!

What do humans do to keep clean?

Humans pour brightly-coloured, gooey, soft potions onto their un-feathered skin. These

have fascinating names, such as 'jojoba &
elderflower'. Apparently, they smell very nice.

Geese have no sense of smell, but I really
look forward to enjoying these luscious smells
and moisturising my REAL human skin!! Us
poor geese have to bathe in the mucky River
Thames. I am pretty sure I saw a human wee
into it last night after drinking too many beers
— EURGHHH!

Gus scanned his rough notes, feeling extremely
pleased with himself. But something was niggling
at him. He scratched his head feathers with his foot
and furrowed his brow. Something about that scary
bully that wanted to make him into a breakfast
sausage... Now what on earth was it? *THINK, GUS,
THINK*, he told himself, scratching his feathers so
hard he nearly poked his brain out with his foot.

Oh, WOW! Could it be? Cherry Blossom Farm?
Surely not – it was too much of a coincidence! But
it must be true! Last night, those ghastly men were
talking about their failed robbery attempt – they
were the thieves that Grandad had outsmarted all
those years ago! And now they were planning to
do something MUCH, MUCH WORSE. If *only*
he could stop them, he would be just like his hero:
Grandad. And if he was a hero, Grandad would be
so proud of him. Then he would DEFINITELY want
to introduce him to Mr Goosman.

NINE

GUS'S MASTERPLAN

Mission Human

by Gus the Canada Goose

41

TEN

GOOSE WIFE, GOOSE LIFE

'Gus! *There* you are! Where *have* you been all day? You've been avoiding me again, haven't you? And what *is* that noisy, rustling sound you're making over there?'

'Er… nothing, Mum,' he mumbled, facing away from her as he dug a hole in the grass with his beak to bury and hide Boris Bacon's notepad in. He needed to keep his big plan to become human secret from Mum and Dad for now. If they found out, they would never understand and just try and talk him out of it. He'd leave that problem until a different day.

'Remember Dad's important meeting I told you about last week? You know, the one to outline the Prime Goose selection process? Well, we must have a quick dinner tonight before making our way to it,' she honked, dipping her beak into a gross mixture of grass, grains and leaves every so often to stir them.

'Uh huh,' grunted Gus, as he kicked mud back on top of the notebook with his webbed feet.

'Are you listening to me at all? I said – REMEMBER THAT IMPORTANT MEETING YOUR DAD IS HOSTING?'

'*Arghhhh*,' Gus hissed, properly paying attention now.

Mum had told him about it, but he had better things on his mind than the boring old *Annual Goose Meeting*. He knew this meeting was important to his family. Dad had been Prime Goose for a while and wanted to retire now to float up and down the river flirting with lady geese. Everyone could see Mum was desperate for Gus to take over – she was so *obvious* it was cringeworthy.

'Grandad came over this afternoon for a cup of river water and mentioned that he told you the whole story of how he and Granny Goosietta met. You probably don't realise this, Gus, but Canada geese can be extremely unpleasant when another type of goose tries to join their flock. They act like complete thugs! Unlike elegant, domestic Chinese geese like your granny was. I'll have you know that when your grandparents first arrived here carrying me as a baby, the whole flock crowded around us with their wings spread out in a cocky, aggressive manner! One *even* pointed his beak at your grandad and hissed, "Come and 'ave a go if you think you're 'ard enough," in a cockney honk!'

'Stop making stuff up Mum. All geese are complete wimps. Cuthbert cried yesterday because he didn't like the dinner his mummy made him, and just last week, Thomasina had a major meltdown because she wasn't happy with how her head feathers were styled on her head! Apparently, she spent ages preening them to look her best – I sure hope all the rumours about her fancying me are lies!'

'Oh yes, Thomasina – thanks for reminding me. That was the other thing I wanted to talk to you about—'

'Oh, not again, Mum—'

'I've seen the way her eyes sparkle when she talks to you. Now you would make a fine Prime Goose with her at your side as your wife. Yes, she's a bit bossy, but you could do much worse. She comes from a fine family of purebred geese. In fact, their bloodline can be traced right back to when King Charles II introduced the very first regal geese to St James's Park in central London!'

Gus groaned and face planted his wings. Why was it that geese were desperate to get their children married off so young? If he was human, it sounded like he would have years of partying left before he even had to *think* about such a daft idea. And Thomasina would be a nightmare of a goose wife – constantly bossing him around.

As Mum divided the dinner into three neat portions, he pulled himself upright and painted a fake smile on his beak before she turned around. The unmistakable shadow of Dad loomed large and Gus figured it was nearly time to go.

'Get this tasty meal down your beaks, quick, ganders!' Mum said. 'We must be heading to the meeting soon…'

Gus sighed. He loved his parents really, and didn't want to disappoint them, but he didn't want to be Prime Goose, and he definitely didn't want to marry Thomasina. They most certainly did not fit into his plan to become human.

ELEVEN

THE AGM
(ANNUAL GOOSE MEETING)

'Doesn't your father look important up there,' Mum honked, loud enough for all the South West London Flock of geese to turn and watch Gus's reaction. 'He's *just* as handsome as the day we met. You know, my darling boy, that'll be you up there very soon...'

'Shh, shut up, Mum!' Gus hissed, jabbing her in the ribs. 'You're *so* embarrassing! Now everyone's staring at us.'

'YOUR MUMMY FANCIES YOUR DADDY, NAH NAH, NAH, NAH NAH!' sang Cuthbert, flying around in little circles of glee.

'Of course she does, you plonker!' hissed Thomasina, biffing Cuthbert with her beak. 'He's her husband! Something *I* plan on having very soon!'

'Children, QUIET!' honked Dad, shooting a disapproving glance in Gus, Thomasina and Cuthbert's direction. He was perched on an elevated stone nicknamed Prime Goose Point. This gave him a good view of the whole flock, like he was the teacher and they were a bunch of naughty children.

'Welcome!' Dad bellowed. 'Now as you know, I have called this meeting to announce my retirement as Prime Goose, the leader of your flock. And...'

There was a drum roll sound in the background as Dad's trusty team of minions flapped their wings to build up excitement. '...to tell you all how YOU TOO could become the NEXT... PRIME... GOOSE!'

Surveying the crowds, Gus saw all the goose families were looking up at Dad, their eyes sparkling with admiration. If only they knew what a twit he was at home, with his self-important flapping wings and stupid jokes that weren't even funny! He had no idea why Mum even married him in the first place.

'Now I'm going to begin with a little story…'

Oh no, please, please, please don't let it be the story about how Dad had single-handedly fought off a large queue of handsome ganders to win Mum's wing in marriage. It was so corny Gus was practically sick in his beak every time he heard it.

'Now, as you all know, the position of Prime Goose was created many years ago. This was because back then, we Canada geese were sadly seen as PESTS! So, the nasty humans kicked us out of our woodland homes into the cities. But we geese made the best of it, as we always do.'

Stop chatting rubbish as usual, Dad, thought Gus. *Humans are awesome, don't diss them.*

'In the cities, we geese have thrived, with a huge increase in numbers of city goose types like ourselves!' continued Dad.

'Listen to what Dad's saying, Gus, it's important,' Mum hissed at him through the side of her beak.

'As a result, a gaggle of geese from this area thought of a super idea: to choose JUST ONE AWESOME goose to lead the larger flock. In fact, having a Prime Goose here worked so well, geese all over the WORLD heard about it and copied us by choosing their own *Prime Geese!'*

'Hear, hear!' honked the rest of the flock, dipping their beaks in water before raising them to toast the success of the 'Prime Goose' role.

Looking around at the admiring glances the other geese were throwing in Dad's direction, Gus rolled his eyes.

'Now before I tell you all the very important information about how you, YES YOU, could become the next Prime Goose, I shall tell you a little story about how times have changed since I became leader. It involves my mother- and father-in-law, the great Granny Goosietta and OG.'

'We cannot wait, dear Leader Goose,' chorused a few middle-aged lady geese, looking Dad in the eye whilst preening their feathers. Even Gus was interested now, if the story was about what his granny and grandad did after emigrating to the riverbanks of South West London.

'Just a few short years ago, we lived in very different times. Our flock was territorial and unfriendly to outsiders. Not just other breeds of goose, mind you, but even our own! Who had simply been raised elsewhere! My mother- and father-in-law travelled far from a human farm, arriving at this very river to seek a new life for their young family! Let's just say, they were not exactly welcomed with wide open wings…' Dad paused and looked solemn.

What? thought Gus. Other geese being mean to his beloved grandad? Why on earth would they do that?!

'This very flock hissed, "Get off MY land!", squaring up to them menacingly.' Dad gave an emotional sigh to heighten the drama. It reminded Gus of when he did it at home to show his disappointment.

'However,' he continued, 'in amongst this kerfuffle, when no one was paying attention, a GREEDY fox hovered in the background! Salivating and licking his lips at the thought of a nice, juicy goose for lunch…

'This fox tiptoed towards the fattest gander in our flock: Goostice! Seconds away from biting his head clean off! Luckily, Goosietta noticed just in time and flew at the fox, hissing loudly and biting his behind with her sharp beak, chasing him off…'

Wow. Just *incredible*. So Granny Goosietta was a hero!

'After that, the Canada geese begrudgingly decided to let this family of outsiders join our flock,' continued Dad.

Too flipping right, thought Gus. What a bunch of wimps they were, leaving his poor granny to risk her life to a feral-fanged fox.

Gus saw Goostice grimace as he drifted towards the back of the crowd. He was ancient now, but his mates still hissed with laughter about it.

'Alas,' continued Dad, 'sadly, from then on, it wasn't all plain sailing for OG and his family. Although able to live amongst this flock, they weren't properly accepted immediately. But, over time, change can happen!' exclaimed Dad, his honk full of hope.

'This flock realised the benefits of letting outsiders join! OG was a skilled Guard Goose from his time living on the farm. And Goosietta, a domestic Chinese goose, was genetically suited to protecting us. Chinese geese are confident and imposing to predators – which is why she was so good at saving juicy Goostice! Our new flock members dramatically reduced the number of OUR geese meeting a grisly end at the feral, gnashing teeth of a predator!'

Gus noticed that the smile on Dad's shiny beak was even smugger than usual, as if *he* personally had fought off all those predators.

'Their hard, courageous work did not go unnoticed. To recognise her services to saving the lives of chunky geese, Goosietta was awarded the title of OBE. This stands for Officer of the Most Excellent Order of the Bird Empire. Only the most exceptional birds receive it! We also created a brand-new leadership role for OG – Chief Sentinel Goose.'

Dad smiled enthusiastically before continuing.

'As you know, we've had sentinels – geese taking turns to guard the flock through the night – since the beginning of time. But we made the role official! OG became the first ever right-hand military gander to protect the former Prime Goose – my late father, Goosebert II. As a result, OG's family has become the most important family in this flock – EVER!

'Before I move on to the Prime Goose election process, I shall raise a toast to the late Goosietta, a loving mother to Goosabella, who she raised as the most amazing, kind-hearted goose! As you all know, I was lucky enough to fight a long queue of ganders to get Goosabella to marry me!'

Typical, thought Gus. *I knew he'd get that in somehow.*

'HEAR, HEAR,' the congregation honked euphorically. 'To the late Goosietta, OBE.'

As the older geese toasted Granny, Gus noticed from the corner of his eye that Thomasina and her gaggle had flown into a huddled circle. He waddled sideways to listen.

'*SO...* who do you think'll be Prime Goose?' hissed Thomasina. 'I reckon Gus. He's *so dreamy...*'

'Rubbish,' honked Evangeline, her beak pointed upwards. 'He's a complete weirdo, all he talks about are human beings. The other day I *actually* saw him spying on them through windows. It's all very strange if you ask me.'

Dad looked in their direction, warning them to pay attention. 'Now, let's take a five-minute break before we reconvene...'

TWELVE

WHO CAN BE LEADER?

Further down the riverside, Gus heard familiar voices.

'Do you mind if I go to Clara's, Dad? She wants to show me her new animal book,' said Boris.

'I couldn't care less, Son, as long as you're back in a couple of hours when your mum comes to get you,' replied Bruce Bacon. 'Be here! I want to avoid her, otherwise that wasp-chewing old witch will wring my neck for more of my hard-earned cash to pay for all that food you shovel in your fat gob.'

*

Dad flew back up to the podium, cleared his throat and looked meaningfully in Gus's direction.

'Lady Geese and Ganders, we meet again for the part you have all been waiting for: the Prime Goose election details.'

Gus saw his flock frantically flap and scuttle around to find their position in the crowd, ready to listen carefully. They were like a bunch of lovesick fans at a pop concert.

'This is a very simple process. BUT... it will ensure that the next leader elected is the highest quality goose for this important job! As this flock is a meritocracy, meaning every goose is important, regardless of background or breeding, anyone, and I mean ANYONE, can compete to be Prime Goose. Of course, this abolishes the old rule that says only male, purebred Canada geese can be chosen for this great honour.'

Gus heard excited murmurs arise from the crowd. He knew some lady geese aspired to be more than just a mother goose and had dreamt of this change. They might not have big dreams to become a completely different species, like him, but they were ambitious as far as being a boring goose could take them.

'What twaddle!' hissed Goostice, who was still in a bad mood from Dad reminding everyone earlier that evening about Goosietta saving his fat behind from the fox. 'A lady can't be Prime Goose! Ladies are far too silly for important jobs and should just stay on their river patch looking after goslings!'

The lady geese looked at him and hissed, 'We have no time for your stuffy old-fashioned ideas,

Goostice! Goosietta should've just let that fox munch you!' honked one loudly.

'Ladies! Ladies! We may not all agree with one another, but we are a friendly flock that is kind to everyone. Now be quiet and let me finish,' Dad boomed. 'For anyone who wishes to take on this great privilege and responsibility, you must write a short speech on what it means to you to be elected Prime Goose. You will then have ten minutes only to give your speech. The date of these speeches is exactly one month today, so you have plenty of time! Your speech will be made to a selection panel of the most powerful ganders in the flock.'

Eurghh, no way can I be bothered with that, thought Gus.

'Then,' continued Dad, 'over the next few days, my selection panel will choose a shortlist of just two geese! The chosen two must come up with a slogan that describes what style of leadership they will provide as Prime Goose, before each making a speech in front of the entire flock. This speech will include a quick explanation of the top-three changes they will make to life in our flock within their first year as Prime Goose!

'Now are there any questions?' Arranging his beak into a wide, cheesy grin, Dad ploughed on before anyone else could get a honk in.

'It's been a real honour to serve this community. But I most definitely could not have done it without my family. I would like to welcome them onto the podium, so we can all toast my brilliant wife, Goosabella, and my son, Gus, of whom we are both very proud!'

But Gus didn't hear Dad's request to join him on Prime Goose Point for a toast. If he flew quickly, he should just about catch up with Boris to see where he was off to and who this Clara was. He suspected it would be an excellent opportunity to find out about different kinds of human life…

THIRTEEN

IT BIT ME, IT BIT ME!

Ding dong!

The doorbell of Clara's pretty riverside house rang, as Boris stood on the doorstep, fidgeting with his chubby fingers in excitement. Peering through the windowpanes on the front door, he could see her bouncing down the stairs to greet him.

'Eeeeee!' came an excited squeal. 'I've been so excited about our playdate I've been literally planning what we could do ALL DAY!' She wrapped her dainty arms around his sturdy neck, almost squeezing out the greasy, ketchup-covered sausage sandwich that Bruce begrudgingly made him for lunch.

'I've been dead excited all day too. Dad's flat is sooo boring. There's nothing to do except listen to him bullying poor Uncle Spike. And I wish he'd buy some different snacks from the supermarket as well

– I like sausages, but I get a bit bored of eating them at EVERY meal!'

Clara giggled. 'I'd *love* sausages at every meal, that'd be super! Mum's always nagging me, "Eat your greens, Clara, eat your greens!" Anyway, come upstairs! I've got something *dead* exciting to show you!'

Boris bounded up the stairs, following Clara's lead.

'Is this new?' he asked, picking up a luminous pink pillow covered in sequins and shaped like a goose.

'Yep!' Clara shrieked. 'It's cool, isn't it?'

'Err, yes, and, er, very pink,' Boris replied, thinking that ever since the gosling hatched in Clara's hands, she'd become goose-obsessed, and it was going a bit too far now. He suspiciously eyed the cream bedspread with pink geese all over it and the fake lit-up goose masquerading as a bedside lamp.

'You know Mum and I are absolutely crazy about geese! Well, she's got this really cool project at work. They're designing something called a Goose Virtual Reality Simulation.'

'Awesome!' said Boris. 'Is it gonna be used for a children's video game or something? I don't know many games where the player would want to be a goose! I'd rather be a superhero.'

'Nah, mostly for schools and museums. So we can learn what it's like being a real wild bird!'

'*No way,*' said Boris in disbelief.

'Yes way.' Clara smiled. 'But guess what! Mrs Trotter has convinced her to come into school and get us all to help with it during art class. We're going to draw some ideas of what people might see when they try on the goggles. Then Mum's going to write the code to make it work. I mean, how embarrassing is that! She only agreed because Mrs Trotter gave her an expensive bottle of wine and a nice card asking her to help. Grownups are so sneaky, the way they give each other wine to bribe each other to do stuff!'

'Nah, I think it's cool. At least your mum's smart and good at stuff besides eating sausages and doing burglaries – and my dad can't even get that right,' sighed Boris.

'Anyway,' said Clara, changing the subject to cheer Boris up, 'let me show you my new book.' She picked up a glossy paperback from her well-stacked wooden bookshelf.

'*What Your Goose Is Thinking,*' Boris read aloud, 'by Siegfried F. Goosman.'

'Look! It has pictures of every type of goose you could imagine. It says on the front it's written based on fact, but Mum and I think that's a joke! Of course, no one knows what a goose is thinking!'

'Let's read to each other! We can put on funny voices too, like we do in drama!'

'Super idea,' Clara replied. 'I look forward to you telling me all about what a goose is thinking!'

'Hang on…'

'What?'

'Can you hear that noise?'

'What *are* you talking about, Boris?!'

'THAT noise! It sounds like a wild goose trying to break into your bedroom window with its beak!'

'Don't be ridiculous, why would a goose want to get inside a human house? It's probably got much funner things to do, like fly and eat mud! Now come on, read!' Clara ordered. 'I want to know how you can tell what your goose is thinking!'

Flicking through, Boris selected a strangely titled chapter and began reading…

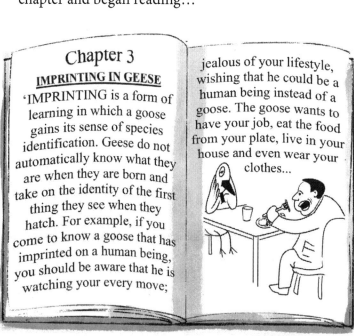

Chapter 3
IMPRINTING IN GEESE

'IMPRINTING is a form of learning in which a goose gains its sense of species identification. Geese do not automatically know what they are when they are born and take on the identity of the first thing they see when they hatch. For example, if you come to know a goose that has imprinted on a human being, you should be aware that he is watching your every move; jealous of your lifestyle, wishing that he could be a human being instead of a goose. The goose wants to have your job, eat the food from your plate, live in your house and even wear your clothes…

'Clara, Boris, come down soon,' yelled Mrs Stecker, Clara's mum, from the sitting room. 'You said you wanted to watch *The Little Mermaid* again with Boris. If you don't start it soon, you won't have time before I need to drop Boris off at his dad's.'

'Hi, Mr and Mrs Stecker, lovely to see you,' Boris said politely as they trundled into the living room.

'Hi, Boris,' said Clara's dad. 'You can call us Sarah and Tom, you know, we're not your school teachers.'

'Of course, of course,' Boris stammered, hoping he hadn't offended them. He'd forgotten that grownups sometimes prefer being called by their first names as it made them feel less ancient.

Clara's dad Tom had some interesting things spread out on the sitting room table, and Boris wondered what they were. One was a pile of pretty-coloured stones, and another was a hefty pile of paperwork.

'What's that, Mr Stecker – sorry, I mean, Tom?'

'Well, this a pile of rare gemstones. We're working on some new designs for my jewellery shop and I thought they'd make nice necklaces. And this, here, is a load of information on the latest security systems to stop burglars stealing expensive stuff from your shop. You can't be too careful these days, you know, especially after that recent million-pound heist in Hatton Garden.'

No, you can't, thought Boris. Especially with people like his dad and Uncle Spike around.

'Stop chatting about that boring stuff,' whinged Clara, getting a bit impatient. 'Can we just watch *The Little Mermaid* now? Pwetty pwease!'

*

'Oh, I love this bit, it's so romantic!' Clara smiled, as the mermaid with the red hair kissed the prince and turned into a human in the prettiest of white wedding dresses. 'Is that what your wedding dress was like, Mum? Did it have princess lace all over?'

Boris was glad the film was over; he was happy to watch it because Clara was his best friend and he knew she loved it, but next time it was *definitely* his turn to choose! Just as Clara's mum was about to answer, something went BANG at the windowpane…

'What on earth was that?' cried Tom, as they all rushed outside to find out.

'Oh no, disaster, Mum! Look! I think this wild goose flew into our window by mistake.' She looked down at the poor creature, lying unconscious on the floor, her brow furrowed with worry. She picked it up and cradled it, gently stroking its feathers as it lay motionless in her arms.

'Clara, I wouldn't do that if I were you…' said her mum in horror.

'It's okay, Mum, I've held a goose before,

remember?! That one hatched in my hands in the park when I was eight!'

Boris watched as the strangest thing happened. The goose gained consciousness and looked lovingly up at Clara before leaning in for a kiss…

'Arghh, IT BIT ME, IT BIT ME, IT BIT ME!' Clara shrieked, dropping it like a hot potato. 'That horrible, mean goose bit my nose!'

FOURTEEN

THE PLAN PROGRESSES

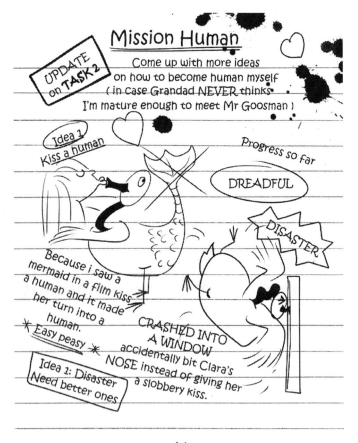

Mission Human

Come up with more ideas
on how to become human myself
(in case Grandad NEVER thinks
I'm mature enough to meet Mr Goosman)

UPDATE on TASK 2

Idea 1
Kiss a human

Progress so far

DREADFUL

DISASTER

Because i saw a mermaid in a film kiss a human and it made her turn into a human.
* Easy peasy *

CRASHED INTO A WINDOW
accidentally bit Clara's NOSE instead of giving her a slobbery kiss.

Idea 1: Disaster
Need better ones

Gus sat doodling little hearts around task two of his masterplan. He was in *lurve*. Not the gross, icky kind of love that Mum felt about Dad, but that lovely, comforting kind that you felt for your own mummy! His real mummy – Clara. *Ahh*, he sighed, thinking of her beautiful, kind, little face.

Gus couldn't believe that he'd found her! The most special human! The lovely little girl whose hands he'd hatched into all those goose years ago. And purely by chance, something he wasn't expecting. It was fate! A sign from the universe that he was on the right track in life: working towards becoming a human himself and living with his Real Human Mummy... *Clara*. Trouble was, he'd discovered that 1) Clara clearly didn't recognise him as her precious son, and 2) humans didn't like being kissed by geese. Maybe he could write her a letter explaining! His handwriting was getting awfully good.

Anyway, he must focus on his mission – becoming human was THE priority! Time for Plan B – kiss another human! This time, he needed someone so stupid, they wouldn't notice a thing if a goose swooped right in and planted a slobbery kiss on their lips...

FIFTEEN

FART FOG

#me&mygorgeousbrucey

Bruce Bacon lay on a tropical beach with a gorgeous lady by his side. They sipped fruity cocktails with little paper umbrellas in. She wore a gold bikini and an engagement ring with a diamond the size of a golf ball. Behind them was their mansion with a beachside view. Tonight, they were having a party for their rich and powerful friends: pop stars, original gangsters and footballers. Taylor Swift would get a gorgeous girly friend to take a photo with her expensive iPhone, before posting it on social media captioned #me&mygorgeousBrucey—

'So, Bruv, what do you want me to do?' asked Spike in his dumb voice, abruptly shaking Bruce out of his delicious daydream.

'Get off that bony backside and get me a beer from the fridge for starters. Leave the important brain work to me.'

'Err, Bruv, before I gets your beer, I fink I need to tell you somefing… There's one of 'em gooses from the river over at the window. It's puckering its beak at me like it wants to give me a big, juicy kiss!'

'IF YOU SO MUCH AS MENTION THE G-WORD AGAIN, I'LL SIT ON YOUR HEAD AND SQUASH YOU INTO THE GROUND UNTIL THERE'S NOTHING LEFT BUT DUST!'

'Honest, Bruv – you need to hear this… Please don't get angry, but it just gave you a cheeky wink like it was taking the mickey or somefing.'

'Don't be so flippin' ridiculous! Get my beer and get it NOW. I'm working on my new business venture and I don't need your idiotic chat distracting me from my genius ideas. This is THE crucial piece of the puzzle to pull off the jewellery heist of the century!'

Bruce jotted down his business plan on a piece of notebook paper. Although smart, he was very impatient and had handwriting like a drunk spider had danced across the page.

This was it. This was the plan that would finally make him as rich as he deserved. He would be on that beach sipping cocktails in no time. Bruce 1, Goose 0!

Big Brucey's big smart business venture

PROBLEM

The best jewellery shops (and i intend to burgle the best) have super security systems. They are so good that even clever-clogs me wouldn't know how to outsmart them – and i am the SMARTEST gangster in London. I spent YEARS in prison over dry bread and watery porridge debating the best ways to outsmart these systems with other smart gangsters (NOT SPIKE !) Not a single one of us with all our super brain power knew how !

SOLUTION

Develop my own security system ! Then i will know exactly how to get past it ! It's also a GENIUS way to FIND OUT which shops have the most valuable jewels – crucial information for the jewellery heist of the century !!

THIS TIME – THERE WON'T BE A GHASTLY GOOSE IN SIGHT !!!!!!

'There you go, Bruv,' said Spike, handing his brother the cold beer. Bruce lifted his head from the business plan that he was scribbling and grunted.

'As you know, or more likely SHOULD know if you had been paying attention, we are developing one of those smoke-based security systems. I did some research and they are what *all* the expensive jewellers have these days,' announced Bruce.

'Smoke? Like what comes out of 'em fags that you and I used to smoke as school boys?' asked Spike.

'NO, IDIOT! Not that kind of smoke. What I meant, is, a thick type of smoke just like fog. When a burglar sets off a security system, the fog billows in huge, thick clouds around the burglar, so he can't see his own arms in front of his face, let alone the item he is trying to steal.'

'But why would we want anyone to 'ave something like that?' asked Spike.

'Flippin' 'eck,' replied Bruce angrily. 'I have explained this to you a *million* times already. As *we* are building the security system ourselves, we will build something that just *we* can get past, to steal all that lovely, lovely jewellery!'

'Oh!' said Spike. 'Bruv, you is genius! But… why would someone want to use our security system instead of one of 'em others sold in the shops?'

'Wow. I cannot believe it! For once a complete muppet like you has asked an intelligent question! Well… I shall tell you how!' said Bruce. 'To get people to buy something from you, it has to have something different and special about it to make people *really* want it!'

'Oh, uh, I get it,' said Spike, grinning goofily and scratching his head with confusion.

'Now I have thought long and hard about this, but I have decided that our *special thing* is going to be "smell"!' Bruce declared proudly. 'Instead of releasing a cloud of thick fog that stops the thieves from seeing the jewels, *our* security system is going to blast out an invisible smelly fog that's so ghastly, the thieves will collapse onto the floor, puking up all their guts, wishing they had never been born!'

Bruce smiled to himself. 'Security systems that blast out thick fog, stopping burglars from seeing the expensive jewellery, may prevent them from stealing it, but then they can still run away! But... if a fantastically foul smell is released instead, the thieves will be so ill they roll around on the floor, in bucket-loads of their own puke! And this means they cannot escape, so the filthy police can come and capture them!'

'Ooh,' said Spike, 'what kind of smell will it be?'

'We need to create a farty smell,' replied Bruce, deadly serious. 'It needs to be as repulsive and sickening as can be.' He grinned, thinking of how to explain it to Spike in a way that he would understand. 'Remember Ciggy Cheryl, your minging girlfriend at school? You know, the one who always reeked of fags?'

'Ooh, yes,' said Spike, smiling fondly at the memory of the only girl who had gone near him at school. His cheeks blushed bright pink, a pleasant change from their usual ghostly hue. 'Ooh, so that's why she was nicknamed Ciggy Cheryl, cause she reeked of fags, innit!'

'Yes,' Bruce sighed. 'Remember how she used to spray about a million sprays of perfume all over herself to try and hide the smelly whiff? Using that fake Chanel No. 5 perfume that her old man picked up off the back of a lorry? And how it never worked because instead she just smelled like a mixture of fags and cheap perfume?'

'Ooh, now come to think of it, she did smell a bit funny,' said Spike, with a pained expression, remembering how Ciggy Cheryl smelt when they were slobbering all over each other's faces behind the school bike sheds.

'Well, that perfume she wore, like all perfumes that the ladies can buy… a lot of hard work goes into making the smell. People who think they are dead clever wear white overalls in laboratories, spending *ages* mixing ingredients and chemicals to create just the right kind of smell! So, in a way, that's what we'll be doing. But, instead of making a nice smell, we'll be creating something that smells utterly repulsive! And we may have to try a few things to get it just right!'

'But hang on, Bruv… when we try and thieve them jewels, won't we end up puking our guts up?

Me doesn't much like the sound of that, I don't eat much food to puke back up, so I'm worried I'll puke up my stomach and brains instead!'

'There's not much chance of that happening, you ain't got no brains in the first place.'

'Well, that's alright then!' said Spike, looking relieved.

Bruce groaned with frustration. 'You see, Spike, this is where the true genius of my spectacular plan comes in! We shall be basing the smell on one of my very own farts! As we are so used to smelling them day in, day out, the ghastly smell won't affect us! It will just make everyone else ill!' Bruce exclaimed, smiling proudly.

'But how will we know which of your special kinds of fart smell to use?' asked Spike.

'Remember your fart bottles?'

'That I do, Bruv!' said Spike proudly, remembering how as a young boy, he would fart into a plastic bottle and sniff the inside of the bottle afterwards.

'They were useful weapons to torture my victims with. I have fond memories of being in the school playground at lunch. I would select my victim carefully, tie them to a tree with a piece of old rope, then jam one of your open fart bottles up their nostrils. It was an interesting little experiment, seeing how long it took people to puke all over their school uniform. The best one was when weedy little

Brian Turdson produced luminous-yellow puke mingled with snot out of his hairy nostrils!'

'Right, come on!' said Bruce, as he jotted down a bizarre grocery list. 'You've given me an idea – maybe you aren't a good-for-nothing twerp 100% of the time. Just 99.9999999% of the time.'

BRUCE'S GROCERY LIST FOR FART
EXPERIMENTS

A few bottles of water
Cans of Red Bull energy drink
Cabbage
Baked beans
Curry sauce in jar – must be very spicy
Chicken and rice (for curry)
Cheese
Eggs
Sprouts
Onions
Sticky labels
Permanent marker pen

'We need to go on a late-night trip to Tesco. We have supplies to buy.'

'Er, Bruv? Now don't get mad but I really need to tell you somefing. I fink that goose I told you about earlier just flew through the window, kissed me and then escaped!'

SIXTEEN

I KISSED A HUMAN, IT WAS GROSS

'Grandad! Grandad! Grandad! Guess what?' Gus screeched excitedly, flying as fast as his wings would carry him to his grandad's patch of the river.

'What, Gus?'

'I'm human! I did it, I did it, I did it! Why didn't you tell me it was so *easy*? All that nonsense about proving to you I was serious and all that faff about introducing me to Mr Goosman. And all I needed to do was kiss a human and *hey presto*! I *am* one.'

'Gus, what on earth are you talking about? Have you gone stark raving mad?'

'Oh, can't you just be proud of me for once, Grandad, instead of treating me like I'm silly and immature all the time! I took matters into my own hands, kissed a human and now I am one!'

'Gus, I hate to break it to you, but you're still a goose.'

'Oh, don't be so ridiculous. I saw it on TV!'

'Saw *what* on TV?'

'When you kiss a real human, you turn into one! Simple!'

'Where on earth did you get THAT idea?'

'I saw two human children through a window watching a film about a creature that looked half-human half-fish kiss a prince – and the creature turned into a REAL human lady!'

'Oh, Gus, Gus, Gus. That's a film called *The Little Mermaid*. It isn't real. Sarah back at the farm used to do some babysitting for local human children. She often watched that film with them, so I know it well. It's just a fun made-up story. It isn't real.'

'Hang on…' Gus paused and looked down at his feathers, wings, skinny legs and webbed feet as the realisation dawned on him. 'You're still a goose,' Grandad had said. The words were like a sucker punch to his feathered midsection. STILL… A… GOOSE…

ARGHHHHH!

He dipped his beak in the River Thames, opened it, swilled a load of water inside his mouth and spat it out like projectile vomit across the other side of the river, before swilling and repeating the action. He'd kissed Spike's mealy, minging mouth for nothing! Nothing!

'Gus, what ARE you doing? Stop that spitting. It's rude. I'm never introducing you to the esteemed Mr

Goosman if you insist on doing ridiculous things like that. You're acting like a complete delinquent. STOP IT.'

Gus burst into tears.

'What's wrong, Gus? I meant stop spitting. Not stop spitting and start crying.'

'I… I… I… I kissed a man and it was gross,' Gus stuttered, heaving out his words in between sobs. 'I thought it would turn me into a human. But it didn't. And so I did it for nothing! And it was… urgh. Just, URGH URGH URGH! I was so excited I didn't even realise it hadn't worked until YOU pointed it out to me.'

'Oh, Gus. Never mind,' said Grandad, softening his tone so as not to upset him further. 'It was just a silly misunderstanding. Look, chin up. We have a plan, don't we? Remember your mission that I set you? You just need to stick to researching humans for now instead of swapping saliva with them.' Grandad smiled. 'One step at a time. And…' he laughed, patting Gus on the back and winking at him, 'if you do insist on kissing a human ever again, just find one that you fancy next time, okay?'

SEVENTEEN

WHAT NEXT?

So, kissing a human was a no-go. That plan failed spectacularly. Gus needed a new plan and he needed one fast. He was getting increasingly fed up with his boring goose life and Mum bossing him about. And Grandad still clearly thought he was an idiot after the spitting incident – there was *no way* he'd introduce him to Mr Goosman anytime soon. Mum always told him not to put his eggs all in one basket. Now was the time to take her advice (for once!). He needed new ideas to transform himself, and he needed them pronto. It was why he found himself wide awake at midnight thinking.

Suddenly, Gus had a flash of genius. He remembered overhearing Clara tell Boris about some project her mum was working on with children at her school. Something called a Goose Virtual Reality Simulation (whatever that was!). Apparently, it let humans try out being a wild bird. If it could do this… then surely… it could do the opposite and turn a goose into a human! Pen poised in beak, he began updating his trusty plan…

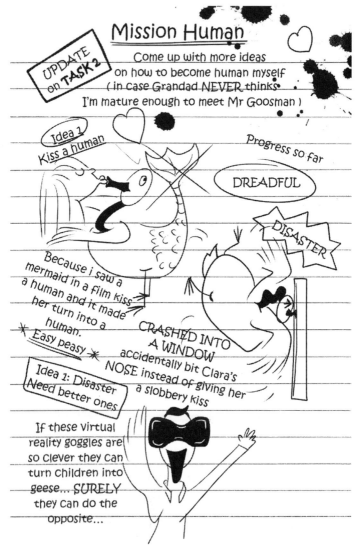

EIGHTEEN

P.S. Clara, I Love You!

'Tap, tap, tap' went Gus's foot on Clara's doorstep the next morning. He was impatient as this was his second big chance to become human and he could not risk missing her departure; he must follow them! There was another good thing about stalking Clara at her school – he could give her the letter that he'd stayed up all night writing (in his neatest handwriting, of course!).

He opened his beak wide and yawned. Where were they?! This was literally taking for *ever*. Oh well, might as well use the time! He unravelled his letter with his beak and gave it one final read-through out loud.

Dear Clara,

I'm writing this letter because you have made me very sad. You've obviously forgotten, so I think I need to remind you that YOU are my REAL mummy. Now I know this will come as a shock to a ten-year-old girl, as humans don't have children until they are ancient and boring, let alone have geese for babies! But it's true. You ARE my real mummy, and I feel so rejected by you I think I shall shrivel up into a ball of feathers and cry and cry.

Now I expect you are wondering how you became mummy to a baby goose at such a young age! Well, let me explain. One summer's day, you were playing in the playground. A goose egg — MINE — rolled down a hill and into the play area. It must be fate. You picked it up and tried to find my mum and dad, but it was too late: I hatched into your hands.

Now you should KNOW that the rules of the goose kingdom are that whoever a bird sees first is its REAL mummy. So that's you. And quite frankly, I'm fed up of the goose that thinks she's my mum — all she does is NAG. She doesn't understand me. So, I'm planning on moving in with you soon. But don't worry, Clara, I'll be human then, so you don't have to worry about me pooing in your bed.

Anyway. You clearly don't remember that magical moment when I hatched in your hands, because otherwise, you would have known that I was just trying to give you a loving kiss the other day. I'm a nice goose, and would NEVER EVER bite my real, human mummy. I hope you find it in your heart to remember me.

Yours lovingly,

Gus (your human-to-be son)

Xxxxxxxxxxxxxxxxxxxxxxx

P.S. Clara, I love you!

'Bye, girls – I hope the science project goes well! Be good for your mum, Clara,' Tom called out.

'Oh, do you have to do this at my school, Mum? Like, really? This is gonna be so embarrassing, my life will be over!' whined Clara.

Finally, thought Gus. He took off, following them, letter tucked neatly beneath his wing, ducking and diving to avoid detection.

'Eurghh,' shrieked a lady in a nice dress and fancy hat. 'It's a Canada goose, it just flew into my hat!'

'Arghhh... yuck... disgusting... urgh... feral creature,' screeched the lady's equally posh friend. 'Vermin! Canada geese are the rats of the bird world – disease-ridden pests.'

Continuing to follow Sarah, Gus flew down the stairwell into the underground tube train station. Now he had to be careful not to fly too close to the kind of humans who looked as if they would kick up a fuss about coming nose to beak with a goose. With Clara and Sarah now underground, he began walking amongst the human feet. Not being able to fly so high indoors, this was the best way to remain unseen. He made himself as short as possible by rolling his neck from its usual upright position into a horizontal one – as if he were half-goose, half-snake.

He'd seen human shoes from a distance, but wow, never this close. Ooh, there were so many different styles. One lady wore pink high heels with silver bows. He *loved* these but wasn't sure if they'd suit him.

The train came into the station and Gus snuck furtively through the doors. 'YEEEOWWWWW,' he felt himself start to honk, as a chunky platform shoe stepped on his tail feather. He quickly cut his large squawk to a mousy squeak, realising just in time that he would be discovered if he made loud noises. Instead, Gus limped on, cursing and hissing under his breath.

Why do the humans look so flippin' miserable on the way to school or work? They had such exciting lives – it made no sense. When his gaggle, the South West London Flock, travelled together in their V-shape, there was constant happy honking – and they had incredibly boring lives. The train humans looked a bit like Mum when she was angry with him. MUM! He'd almost forgotten about her. She'd been in bed when he arrived last night and when he left this morning. When she finally got her sharp beak into him she'd be hissing mad – but he must put that to the back of his mind for now and concentrate on the task at hand.

Gus listened to station name announcements as they travelled along. They all had strange, exciting names like 'Gloucester Road'. *If a boring old goose had named it, it would be called something stupid like 'Gooster Road'*, he thought. There also would have been nothing so fabulous-sounding as 'Westminster'. To a stupid goose, that would be 'Nestminster'.

WALLOP!

Emerging from the station, something thwacked him on the side of his beak, knocking him sideways. Gus looked in the direction of the random flying item and saw a fat, male human adult inside a rundown car drive off.

'Measly amount of chocolate. I'll waste to nothing but skin and bones,' Gus heard a familiar voice yell out of the car window, mixed in with lots of very rude words that his mum would clip him round the ear for saying.

Gus looked down. The man had thrown a piece of chocolate cake at him! He took a moment to savour its glorious appearance before vacuuming the entire thing up in one go. It was delicious, with its heavenly, messy, chocolatey gooey-ness! It was the stuff of dreams. He was so consumed with pleasure that he failed to notice Sarah disappearing into the crowds and that a couple of teenage humans were taking photos of him eating his cake.

'Woah! How cool is that! That goose, like, literally ate a whole slice of chocolate cake in one go. I got a super cool pic of him with a cake-shaped bulge in his neck as he swallowed. Man, I'm uploading this to my Insta now,' said the human teenager, whilst typing *#howgreedyisthisgoose #goosegoals #ilovelondonwildlife* into his smartphone.

#howgreedyisthisgoose
#goosegoals
#ilovelondonwildlife

By now, a big crowd had gathered around Gus. He looked up at his audience and put on his best goosey smile. He showed his teeth and waggled his tongue. He stalked around, enjoying being the centre of attention. He flapped his wings – they were loving him! More phones clicked, taking pictures. This was the way to do it. If he were to become one, it was important that humans liked him. Suddenly, Gus realised he couldn't see Clara and Sarah. 'Argh,' he honked. He had got carried away. He spread his wings and took off to look for her, scattering chocolate cake crumbs left, right and centre as he went.

NINETEEN

CLARA'S SCHOOL

Gus saw Sarah's shiny brown hair and goose-pattern dress in the distance, with little Clara, his lovely Human Mummy, by her side. Phew! It only took him a few seconds to catch up with them. They walked towards a huge scary building with a sign saying 'Riverside School'.

'Bye, Mum,' he heard her hiss at Sarah. 'Can you please wait outside *at least* ten minutes before coming in, you're going to completely cramp my style if we walk in together. See ya!'

Brilliant, now he had Clara to himself. He could give his letter to her and finally reveal his identity as her son. Then they could share a special bonding moment in which she'd wrap her arms around him, give him a lovely big kiss and say, 'Oh, Gussy! Can you ever forgive me for forgetting my precious son? I know, come back home with me and I'll bake a big, gooey, super-chocolatey cake with popping candy on top to make up for it...'

He stroked her leg with his flight feather to get her attention.

'Arghhh... what the... arghhhhhhh! It's you again! That animal that bit me! What on earth are you doing following me to school! Get back in the river!'

Gus flashed Clara his best smile and held out the letter with his wing.

Her face softened a little as she unravelled his letter. 'Are you just trying to make friends? Is that all you want? You have a very strange way of going about it, biting me and giving me bits of paper with scribbles on.'

Scribbles? Gus's heart sank. *Maybe humans can't understand goose writing. What a waste of my precious time!*

'Don't look so sad, goose, we can be friends. If you, like, really want to come to school with me, you can. But hide under my jumper, or I'll get in BIG trouble! Once, this girl called Ella Fossington-Smith brought her sister's Persian kitten in for Show and Tell! It drank all the full-fat milk from the school canteen, so Mrs Snipple said no animals, like, ever again!' Scooping Gus up and shoving him under her jumper, she skipped along with the other children into school.

'Children, children!' Gus heard someone shriek from under Clara's jumper. 'Now please shut up and sit down. Barry! I saw you yank Nigel's trousers up his bottom. Five hundred lines in detention for YOU later!'

'Wedgy, wedgy, Nigel's got a wedgy!' came a raucous chant, followed by weird pinging noises and more shouting and laughing.

'I said... SHUT UP! Oh, do SHUT UP and SIT RIGHT DOWN. Did your mothers teach you no manners?' The grown-up voice was getting shoutier as time passed. Gus peeped through a small hole in Clara's jumper, trying to see who owned the shouty voice.

'Sorry, Mrs Trotter,' replied a small human, who didn't sound at all sorry.

Trotter? What a stupid name for a human, Gus thought. He peeked out to get a better look. The shouty voice belonged to a human lady wearing a white blouse covered in paint splashes and a tropical hat. What a silly hat – the woman was in a school classroom to teach a bunch of naughty human children on a rainy morning, not lounging on a beach! And why did that small human next to Barry have his trousers pushed right up his bottom crack? What a ridiculous way to wear trousers.

Mrs Trotter scratched her nails across the whiteboard to get everyone's attention.

'Oh, Miss, did you have to? My ears!' whined little Nigel.

'We need to begin our art lesson, children. We

have a VERY special visitor today – Mrs Sarah Stecker, who also happens to be Clara's mum!'

All the children looked at Clara and smirked. Gus noticed that the skin on her face had turned pink, like his feathers did when Thomasina flirted with him.

'Now, we're very lucky to have Sarah here today, because she's the world's leading goosologist!'

'What the flippin' 'ell is a goosologist?' yelled Barry.

'It's someone who devotes themself to studying the lives and habitats of geese, for the purposes of educating the rest of the world about how to make sure they don't end up dead like the dodo,' piped up Boris.

'Correct, Boris.' Mrs Trotter smiled. 'Ten house points for you! But today, Sarah's here to work on an extremely exciting project with us. As well as being a goose expert, she is also a talented computer programmer!'

'Like someone that makes REAL apps and games like the ones my big sister uses on her phone all the time?' piped up Nigel.

'Yeah, like them dating apps that all them sixth-form girls with the big boobs use,' yelled Barry.

'Do pipe down, Barry,' Mrs Trotter sighed, droplets of sweat running down her face.

'Sarah will be spending the next two weeks here as she needs your help! She's in charge of the

"Feathered Creature Department" at the University of Central London and is developing something very clever... a "goose experience" to use with Virtual Reality goggles!'

'Err, Miss?'

'Yes, Barry,' Mrs Trotter said, looking exasperated.

'Me dad said he had beer goggles on last weekend. Will it be like that?'

'No, Barry, not exactly.'

'Well, what's the point of it, then, Miss? Sounds stupid.'

'When it's finished, Sarah will use it to help biology students learn more about the habitats in which geese live. Then... it will be available in computer shops to buy – so anyone can experience what it's like being a goose – simply by putting on a pair of goggles! So, I guess you could describe it as a video game, where the main character is a wild goose. But you aren't just playing the game, like you would with a remote control or screen. You are actually *in* the game. And YOU... are the GOOSE!'

'Miss, Miss...' yelled Boris, waving his chubby hand in the air.

'Yes, Boris,' said Mrs Trotter, sounding stressed. Gus mentally crossed teacher off the list of Potential Jobs for Him to Have When He Became Human.

'So, like, to explain simply, when someone looks through the goggles, it will be as if you are looking through the actual eyes of a real goose.'

'Yes, Clever Clogs,' Mrs Trotter replied. 'Now for our lesson today, we need to help Sarah with something extremely important! Her and her team of bird scientists have written all the clever code to make the goggles work. Now she needs you to show her what great artists you are! You'll be drawing up ideas of what people might see when they look through the goggles. Now think carefully about this. What would a wild goose that lives by the river see?'

'Probably Bacon's dad taking a big old poo into the river! He's a bit of a wrong un, ain't he, Bacon?'

'SHUT UP, BARRY, you big old horrid bully, leave Boris ALONE,' shouted Clara. Gus felt a flush of pride as his real Human Mummy stuck up for her best friend. He poked his head up from the jumper's neckline to help Clara by giving Barry a menacing glare accompanied by a low, guttural hiss.

'Arghhhh! Miss! Arghhhhhhh! Clara's got a REAL goose hiding under her jumper… arghhh… argh…'

'Don't be so ridiculous, Barry! Stop telling tales.'

'But it's true, Miss! Arghh… it just gave me evils! I think it's gonna attack me, it's squaring up like it wants to fight me…'

The whole class burst into fits of laughter.

'Right. That's IT. I'm not putting up with your behaviour any longer!' screamed Mrs Trotter. 'At the end of class, go and wait outside the headmistress's office. She can deal with you. But now can you please all be quiet and start drawing your ideas of what a real-life goose might see. Think river, think seaweed, think mud, think other geese… and get on with it. Pronto!'

TWENTY

What the Goose Saw...

Gus snuggled back down to remain hidden and began watching activity unfold through the jumper hole again. He didn't want to get Clara in trouble. Mrs Trotter was stalking up and down the class, looking unimpressed as she looked down at the human children's drawings. Using his sharp avian eyesight, Gus had a good look too through the jumper hole.

'What on earth is this, Nigel?' said Mrs Trotter.

'Umm, it's a goose across the other side of the river, Miss.'

'It looks like a lump of poo with feathers stuck in it. *Awful.* Try again!' She picked up Nigel's drawing, crumpled it into a ball and threw it across the classroom into the bin as he promptly burst into tears.

What a goose might see
by Nigel aged 10 + 9 months + 3 days

'This is a *wonderful* drawing, Clara! Would you like to hold it up and tell the rest of the class all about it?'

'Oh yes, Miss! Well, I thought a riverside goose might see other birds – like ducks! You see this one? That one's having a sleep! And these two are a mummy goose and her baby having a swim! Ooh, and that's me, over there, enjoying a super-delicious picnic!'

Picture of what a
Goose might see
By Clara aged 10

'Cheat,' sniggered Barry. 'She only knows how to draw geese cause she brought a REAL one to school to copy!'

'I'll have no more of this goose nonsense, Barry! Seeing as you have so much to say for yourself this morning, would you care to share your picture with the rest of class?'

Barry held up his drawing and the rest of the class fell about in fits of laughter.

stupid picture of what a stupid goose might see drawn in a very stupid art class by Barry aged 10

'Disgrace. You're an UTTER DISGRACE. You can show this to Mrs Snipple at the end of the lesson too. She WON'T be impressed!'

Gus saw Mrs Trotter turn and face Sarah, red-faced with embarrassment. 'What do you think, Sarah? Any good ideas here to use for your goose goggles?'

Sarah smiled, looking doubtful. 'You mentioned that you teach GCSE art too when we first spoke about this project? Well, um, maybe we could let them have a go and see if they could come up with something? I'll bring in the actual goose goggles that day too, and let the older students actually try them out.'

'Excellent plan!' said Mrs Trotter, looking relieved. 'But now, I think I'll take the rest of the day off. I need a cocktail to calm my nerves...'

TWENTY-ONE

THE ART PROJECT

PHEW! That was close.

Gus's original plan had been to stay hidden and not get Clara in trouble, until he'd decided on the best person at school to turn him into a human. It wasn't the class teacher Mrs Trotter – she was an idiot. It probably wasn't Sarah either. True, she was a grownup and could do all the clever coding stuff – so she might *even* be the only capable one. But she was far too sensible, and Gus wasn't sure if she'd be willing to entertain the idea. As for the school children, well, their artwork was awful. If that's what they thought geese looked like, he *definitely* didn't want to find out what they would design a human like, let alone risk letting them turn him into one! Nope, none of them. He had to find another way to come back and find the best person.

But now he had to leave ASAP. There was a danger someone would start believing Barry if he didn't shut his big fat gob. Nor did he fancy spending the rest of the school day heating up in a jumper like roast goose.

Undetected, he quietly flew into Mrs Trotter's hat which provided the perfect camouflage for his escape. As she waited outside school for a taxi, from the top of her head, he read the email which she was frantically typing into her phone.

To: **All Parents of GCSE Art Students at Riverside School**

From: **mrs.trotter.art-teacher@riversideschool.com**

Subject: **Inspiration for New GCSE Art Project**

Dear Parents,

I am emailing you with EXCITING news about a new project which we are introducing into the GCSE Art Curriculum – almost guaranteed to get everyone an A*!

We have joined up with **Dr Sarah Stecker.** Sarah has a **PhD in Goosology** from the University of Oxford, and now teaches at the University of Central London, where she is working on a leading science research project. The goal of the project is to help humans understand what it's like to be a goose in its own natural, wild habitat.

To do this, she and her team are creating a brand-new simulation, called the 'Goose Experience', to be used with VR goggles. Basically, this means that anyone can put on a pair of goggles and know what it's like to be a real, live, ACTUAL goose!

Our request of the GCSE art students is that they draw some ideas of what one might see through the goggles! We kicked off this project with year six (aged 10–11) pupils. However, their artwork was not quite up to the necessary standard. Therefore, we have decided to extend it to GCSE students.

But that's not all! To ensure the artwork is as realistic as possible, students may bring in real-life resources to inspire them. This could be seaweed, mud, a sample of river water, leaves or even… a REAL GOOSE(!).

We will be working on this on Wednesday morning, so please do not forget!

Yours sincerely,
Mrs B. Trotter
Head of Art at Riverside School

TWENTY-TWO

FLAMINGO HAT

Bruce Bacon was driving his taxi out and about in London. It was something he and Spike did to make money, as they were far too rubbish at burglaries to make a living from those. Today had not been his day. First, his early morning snack of chocolate cake had been so disappointing he'd thrown it out of the window. Now, some ghastly customer had just rolled into his cab. She was as tall as she was wide and looked like an apple.

'Aww, thank goodness, I was worried I'd be waiting there all day! I'm Mrs Betsy Trotter,' said the woman, pumping Bruce's hand up and down as if milking an overfed cow.

Bruce snarled and started driving.

'Oh, I've had the most *dreadful* morning, you know. Teaching my awful bunch of year sixes how to draw. Barely a scrap of talent amongst them. Awful things, ten-year-old children. I wish they'd hurry and grow up.'

Bruce grunted knowingly.

'My advice to you? NEVER become a teacher!' said Mrs Trotter.

'Anyway, so this morning, the most vile little blob of a child came up with such a ridiculous lie!' Betsy continued, jabbering on at a million miles per hour. 'That one of his classmates had smuggled a real-life goose into class under her jumper! Now that's right up there with "the dog ate my homework". As if!' Mrs Trotter guffawed. 'You don't get birds in schools.'

'Where would you like to go, Ma'am?' asked Bruce Bacon, wishing this awful woman would shut up.

'Ooh, to The Grand Goose Hotel by Putney Bridge, please. You know the one, overlooks the river. I've just arranged to meet up with some artist friends for an expensive goose egg and cocktail brunch! Figured I might as well relax and enjoy myself after all the stress of teaching one art lesson today!'

Glancing in the rear-view mirror, Bruce thought to himself how ridiculous the woman looked in her flamboyant, tropical hat – exactly the kind of thing he'd expect a crazy art teacher to wear. It had a few Caribbean-style stuffed birds decorating the rim and some exotic pieces of fruit, such as pineapple and papaya. All the pretend birds were brightly coloured, with the exception of one that had grey and black feathers and was noticeably larger than the rest. The hat was quite ridiculous, but if you liked that type of thing – which he didn't – that one bird seriously ruined it. Probably some vile type of Caribbean pigeon. Yuck.

When Bruce arrived at The Grand Goose Hotel, he dropped her off. Before rolling out onto the pavement, she adjusted her hat as if it felt much lighter on her head. Betsy and her flamboyant hat exited the cab. The hat now minus one grey and black feathered bird.

'Thanks, Lovey. Ooh, I almost forgot – here's a nice tip for your troubles,' she said, so wrapped up in her own world that she failed to notice the drops of slobber forming as Bruce salivated over the money.

TWENTY-THREE

BOTTLED FRYED SOSSIDGE

When Bruce Bacon arrived back at his filthy, stinky flat later that day Gus flew out of his cab as fast as his wings would carry him. What a horror of an afternoon! He hadn't much enjoyed pretending to be a hat decoration. It was hard balancing on the rim of Betsy Trotter's hat, particularly as he was much bigger than the pretend flamingos, hummingbirds and parrots. And to make matters worse he kept getting knocked on the beak by a stupid, luminous plastic pineapple.

Keeping well back, he followed Bruce as he walked up the stairwell and through his flat door. Entering the flat was a very risky plan – if he didn't want to become a goose sausage – but he needed to hang around them more to find out exactly what they were up to with this jewellery heist plan. He glided around the edge of the walls like a much-needed feather duster, before settling himself in a hidden corner in the kitchen to observe.

'Right, Dipstick, we don't have much time! I've *already* found a jewellery shop owner who's interested – and we haven't even built the system yet! He arranged a meeting with us this week – if all goes well, he will want to buy it!' Gus heard Bruce say to Spike.

'Uh huh,' said Spike, looking like he couldn't really be bothered with Bruce's plan anymore.

'PAY ATTENTION!' Bruce shouted angrily. 'We can't miss our chance. It's the crown jewel of opportunities, quite literally.'

Gus shuddered as Bruce's evil, raucous laugh boomed through the flat.

'Why, Bruv?' Spike asked, stifling a yawn. 'But there is plenty of other shops wiv expensive things in 'em.'

'I have staked this one out already. It's called "Tom Stecker Jewellery" and it's in Hatton Garden.'

The Tom Stecker Jewellery Shop! Gus was absolutely horrified. That shop belonged to his Human Mummy's family! He absolutely had to stop this! Not only was it important to prove to Grandad how mature he was, but now it was to save Clara's family shop too!

'They have some of *the* most beautiful jewels in their shop and they're worth a fortune! All the rage amongst the celebrities and footballers' wives apparently! There's no other shop as grand as this one! Now, if we get Mr Tom Stecker signed up as our first client, we will only have to carry out one security-system installation to get an eye-watering reward!' Bruce said, his eyes lighting up.

'Whereas, on the other hand,' Bruce spat out, 'if Mr Stecker doesn't want to use our system, I will have to bother going around installing it in a few more shops whilst I spend yet *more* time investigating suitable shops to burgle! You see, Spike, it all comes down to minimum effort, maximum reward! To explain that so that your peanut-sized brain gets it, I mean, doing hardly any work and making tonnes of cash!'

Noticing a dried-out brown morsel on the carpet, he stopped his enthusiastic rant abruptly. It was a chunk of old fried sausage he had dropped on the carpet five years ago. Licking his lips, Bruce picked it up and popped it into his mouth.

'*Gerffff uh ferrfff canfss obth Redth Bullthh duh yuh neckthh,*' Bruce mumbled, his mouth stuffed with ancient grisly sausage mixed with a few carpet hairs.

'Uh?' Spike said sleepily. His afternoon nap was well overdue.

'I SAID… GET A FEW CANS OF RED BULL DOWN YER NECK. What, are you deaf as well as stupid now?'

Spike dutifully did what his brother said. After all, Bruce was the brains of the pair, best not to argue.

'Great,' said Bruce, antique sausage safely inside his fat stomach. 'Now we are going to work through the night to create the most odious smell possible!'

*

First, Gus saw the brothers empty the water bottles to create space for something deadly. Then, Bruce ordered his brother to serve up various foods for him. Spicy chicken curry, eggs, cabbage, sprouts, baked beans, cheese, onions and, of course, fried sausage. After trying each dish, he farted into the empty bottle before screwing the top on tightly. Spike wrote descriptions of what was in the bottle on sticky labels, before proudly sticking them on:

Bottled Cabidge Fart
Bottled Bakd Beenz Fart
Bottled Chikkin Curree Fart
Bottled Cheez Fart
Bottled Egz Fart
Bottled Sprowt Fart
Bottled Unneeun Fart
Bottled Fryed Sossidge Fart

Gus wrapped his wings around his body to restrain himself from a powerful urge to fly right over, snatch the pen from Spike's hand and sort it all out. Even he knew the spellings were wrong, and he was a goose! But this was the least of his worries.

He had to stop the Bacons, he just had to. It was do or die! If he didn't, there'd be no meeting with Mr Goosman, no human transformation, and to top it all off, all those beautiful jewels that belonged to Tom, Sarah and his Human Mummy Clara would be in the hands of evil Bruce Bacon!

TWENTY-FOUR

MOTHER GOOSE TEARS

Flying closer to his riverbank home after his long night spying on the Bacons, Gus saw Mum perched on the grassy verge by the river, hunched over *his* notebook. Tears rolled down her beak like fat raindrops and plopped loudly on the floor. She had it open on the page that read 'Notes on what humans do – by Gus'.

'Mum, what's wrong?' Gus gently asked, approaching with caution.

'You know exactly what I'm crying about – THIS!' She angrily jabbed her beak in the direction of the notebook. 'I found it whilst out hunting for *your* breakfast this morning. It looks like a riverside rat has dug it up and feasted upon it for his breakfast!'

Gus tried to remain calm, not wanting to cause more tears. He couldn't deal with Mum's emotional outbursts. 'But why are you so upset?'

'Your dad and I… we… we… we… Argh, I'm so upset I can't even get my honks out properly! And you've EVEN wrapped Grandad around your stupid, ungrateful wing to get him to help! To think, my own father – a traitor!' Her eyes flashed angrily.

'We work so hard to give you EVERYTHING!' she continued. 'And are you grateful? NO! You're just an immature, greedy goose for whom nothing is ever enough! Do you have ANY idea how hard it was for Granny and Grandad, arriving in this community as complete outsiders? And how hard it was for me, growing up in this judgmental flock as a mixed-breed gosling?! Back then things weren't like they are now, where everyone is accepted despite the colour of their feathers! No! We worked so *hard* to make our family the important one it is in the flock today. To change things for the better! So *you* could grow up and be accepted immediately! So *you* could have a much easier life than I did!'

Mum's feathers were shaking. 'And what do you do? You throw this opportunity right back at us, you ungrateful little gosling. You show no interest in being elected Prime Goose, maintaining the important status this family has achieved and continuing the great work your father and I are doing! No, being a premier goose at the top of the flock pecking order is simply not enough for a precocious gosling-brat like my own son! A goose so arrogant he looks down his beak at the entire flock and even his own SPECIES! You find us and our way of living so tiresome, you think you're above it and want to be something else entirely: HUMAN!' Mum simultaneously spat and hissed the word.

Gus hung his head in shame. He felt terrible that Mum was so upset but couldn't think of anything to say back.

Seconds later, Dad swooped in, looking stressed. Gus took one look at his face and knew Dad was too distracted to pay any attention to him and Mum, so thankfully he was saved from another lecture.

'There's been a bit of a crisis relating to the safety of the entire South West London Flock,' he honked worriedly. 'A gang of foxes living by that block of human flats over there have started circling our territory. News on the riverside is that their current food supply is unreachable. Apparently, they always scavenge sausages from a dirty flat up there, but last night the humans were releasing such toxic fart smells that the foxes can't even bear to sneak in for breakfast. So now they're starving and thinking of chomping down on a goose or two. I must do something to stop it – we can't have another Goostice situation!'

'Oh, it never rains but it pours!' said Mum miserably. She let out a large sigh, raising her beak and wings, before curling up into a feathered ball of dismay.

Dad gave Gus a quizzical look. 'What's wrong with the pair of you? Oh, actually, don't tell me – I don't want to know!'

'No, you certainly don't want to know!' said Mum, shooting Gus a disapproving look. 'I will deal with you later, Gus. For now, though, we must make sure that all *these tiresome geese with lives so dull they aren't worth living* don't meet a grisly end at the fangs of a fox.'

'Mum, don't be so dramatic,' said Gus, pushing his luck. 'I care for the safety of all river geese, even if *you* don't think so.' With that parting shot, he turned his back on his parents and flapped away into the sky.

TWENTY-FIVE

FEATHERED FEMINISM

'Gus, Gus… YOOHOO… wait up for me! I *knew* it was you! We might as well get breakfast together as we're out at the same time this morning!'

Just *great* – Thomasina, of all people. She slowed down her flight speed to a crawl pace before doing three of what she hoped were very elegant circular swoops around Gus's head. Landing herself dramatically right in front of his beak, she raised her wings for maximum impact. Now she was seriously invading his personal space.

'Oh, uh, morning, it's you,' he grunted, hoping she'd get the message that he wasn't in the mood for company.

'Aww, Gus, *sweetie*, why the long beak? A handsome, dreamy gander like you shouldn't be so sad!' He recoiled as she rested a supportive wing gently on his.

'Oh, it's Mum,' he honked. 'She has her feathers

in a twist because I'm not growing up to be the type of son she wants!'

'Oh, rubbish,' said Thomasina sympathetically. 'She's very proud of you and couldn't wish for a finer son!'

'Oh, you just wouldn't *understand* the pressure I'm under! I have such a lot to live up to with my dad being Prime Goose and my grandfather being the original Chief Sentinel Goose,' said Gus, shrugging off her wing.

'Have you started preparing your speech about what it would mean to you to be Prime Goose?'

'Oh, not you as well. All everyone wants to do is have a go at me! But no, I haven't for that matter. I've got other stuff on my mind.'

'Surely you know Cuthbert's been planning his since your dad had the AGM and announced the selection process,' Thomasina continued. 'Having said that, he's only got as far as the first sentence, which goes something along the lines of, "Being Prime Goose would mean loads to me because if I was Prime Goose, I would have lots of hot lady geese queuing up to marry me.""

Gus pulled a face. He didn't rate Cuthbert's chances of being chosen as one of the final two.

'But you should really get started on it, you know, Gus. You wouldn't want Lucinda to beat you.'

'Who on earth's Lucinda? Never heard of her,' he said, dismissively. 'She isn't one of the cool gang.'

'Oh, *Lucy Goosey Gander*,' said Thomasina mockingly. 'She flies with that crowd of lady geese who think that we females deserve more than simply laying eggs and raising our young. We call her Lucy Goosey Gander because she thinks and acts like a gander instead of a lady. Always honking on about something called feminism and how empowering it would be to have a lady as Prime Goose for once!'

Thomasina gazed into Gus's eyes. Gus shifted uncomfortably.

'Anyway, I don't agree with her! We ladies are different from ganders. Prime Goose is an all-consuming job, definitely a gander's work. *I* want enough time to be able to style my feathers so they look just perfect! But the empowerment of lady geese is getting quite fashionable these days. And Lucy Goosey Gander is a very smart lady goose. So, she might do well in the Prime Goose process. You have been warned!'

For a brief second, Gus was interested in listening to more of what Thomasina had to say. Maybe his original thought about Lucinda not being important was too hasty. She sounded quite interesting: wanting something different from what she'd been brought up to expect and doing everything she could to get it. Unfortunately, he didn't get a chance to hear more, as at that moment, his thoughts were baited and switched by a recognisable voice coming from elsewhere…

'C'mon, Spike! We must be at The Grand Goose Hotel for 10am this morning! I have arranged an important meeting with an aromachologist – he's agreed to meet us at VERY short notice for an additional fee, so we absolutely must not be late!'

'An Aroma-Wotsit?' asked Spike, sounding very confused.

For once Gus didn't blame him, he had *no* idea what Bruce was talking about, but he was clearly up to no good.

'I gotta go, Thomasina,' Gus honked abruptly, flying after Bruce and Spike to catch up with them. He turned his back and flew away, exiting so abruptly that he whipped up a ferocious wind, displacing Thomasina's neatly preened feathers.

TWENTY-SIX

The Grand Goose Hotel

Gus flew further down the riverbank, stalking the Bacon Brothers until they came to their venue: The Grand Goose Hotel. Now, he'd heard stories about this place from Grandad. He looked it up and down, marvelling at its beautiful gothic architecture. When he became human, he intended to stay over in many fancy hotels, enjoying the fine dining and sumptuously soft pillows – but he figured he'd give The Grand Goose Hotel a miss – it just sounded a bit too 'goosey'.

Flying towards the revolving doors, he noticed a gold plaque on one of the main turrets. Ever a curious goose, he sidled up to it, reading to himself the ornate old-fashioned writing.

*

The Grand Goose Hotel was built around the year 1680, by a German man named Franz Goosman, who had emigrated in search of adventure. Franz was a writer, who enjoyed taking walks along the River Thames to clear his head and think of ideas for his novels. Soon, he noticed that families of a new type of bird were setting up home along the river. They were avid, feisty and loud, and once they arrived, the riverbank would never be the same again!

Mr Franz Goosman was fascinated by these creatures, which he later discovered were called 'Canada Geese'. They had recently been introduced to the UK by King James in St James's Park, because back then the English ones were a boring grey, whereas the Canada geese were colourful. Like Franz, these birds were adventurous, and many had flown from the park to explore. The geese had decided that they quite liked South West London, as the plants were juicy and the water plentiful. So, they decided to stay put.

To cut a very long story short, Franz's dream was for as many people as possible to enjoy these fabulous birds, for he had fallen quite in love with them! So, he recruited a team to build a grand hotel overlooking the river. The hotel was designed by his team of architects so that as many rooms as possible had a river-facing balcony to enjoy views of feisty, wild geese. He proudly named it 'The Grand Goose Hotel'. It has become something of a Goosman family legacy, passing through generation after generation. The current proprietor is his descendant: a man named Siegfried F. Goosman.

*

Another crazy goose-obsessed family, thought Gus, bracing himself as he flew inside to find the Bacons. But hang on… *Goosman?* Could it be that the owner of this hotel was Grandad's friend, the important Mr Goosman? Surely there couldn't be that many humans around with a name as silly as Goosman! This could be an opportunity to find out more about this special man, the man who one day might be turning Gus into a human being!

To the left of the reception area was a sign that read 'THE GRAND HALL'. Hearing the Bacon Brothers before he saw them, he flew through the doorway in the direction of their voices. On entering The Grand Hall, Gus realised he had a significant advantage for remaining unseen: the place was absolutely *full* of goose paraphernalia. There were china ornaments of geese, elaborate vases with a goose print on, lamps with brass stems in the shape of a goose with an upward-pointing beak… and so it went on. Even the carpet had an old-fashioned goose print woven into the fabric.

Therefore, he had quite a choice when deciding how to camouflage his body. After much hissing and honking quietly to himself in deliberation, he settled on pretending to be a taxidermy ornament.

'Bruv, what on earth is we doin' in this fancy old hotel with gooses everywhere?' Gus heard Spike say, sounding and looking very out of place. 'Couldn't we 'ave gone to Tony's greasy spoon caff for a fry-up instead? You like 'em breakfast sausages there.'

'Keep your voice down, Spike – I will explain everything in a second. We must pretend we are wealthy but obviously law-abiding businessmen, here to have a business meeting,' said Bruce.

'Oh, and what on earth was you doing rustling about at 5.30am this morning? I bet you never even went to sleep, did you, Bruv? I was desperate for some shut-eye after staying up so late making 'em farts, but what wiv your rustling and the rotten pong in the flat it was very hard!' said Spike, stifling a yawn.

'I told you we're short of time and need to get things moving fast,' Bruce growled. 'Now we have produced a sample of repulsive smells, we need a specialist to tell us which one is the most repulsive of all. Then, we need him to manufacture a large volume of this smell for our security system. Well, something that smells identical to whichever of my farts he chooses. I may be able to fart for England, but even I can't produce the amount of smell that's required for the system. Do you have all the bottled sample farts?'

'Oh, that I do,' said Spike proudly. 'Just in this 'ere bag over 'ere.'

'Great,' replied Bruce. 'As you know, our finances are not so good these days, what with all the money we didn't earn during those years in prison. Also

– no one's interested in hiring me to beat up locals from rival gangs. Mad Dog O'Banion wants nothing to do with me since all that goose palaver at Cherry Blossom Farm. He thinks being seen with me will ruin his reputation.'

Spike shuddered at the mere mention of Mad Dog O'Banion. He was hard as nails and even fatter than Bruce. If you so much as looked at him he would stamp you into the ground.

'So,' continued Bruce, 'we don't have much money. To convince the aromachologist to meet us at such short notice, I had to think quick. Luckily, I was able to entice him by suggesting we meet at The Grand Goose Hotel. Everyone's desperate to come here as it's famous for being expensive. They think posting posh posey photos of 'em dining here makes them look dead rich! So, it doesn't come cheap. Especially getting a table at this short notice.'

'So how is we payin' for it then, Bruv?'

'I figured the quickest way to get my hands on cash was to find a city boy, you know, one of those rich banker types, and steal his hard-earned cash. City boys start work early, which is why I went to hover around the Tube station at an unholy hour to pick my victim.'

'Wow, Bruv, I like your thinking! You really *is* genius.'

'Luckily, I managed to find a complete twerp. Poncing around in his expensive suit, thinking he looked quite the part. The idiot also had a few fifty-pound notes in a gold money clip in his back pocket. What a show-off! So arrogant and self-absorbed, bleating into his expensive iPhone, he didn't even notice when I swiped them!'

Bruce gave an evil laugh and Spike joined in, honking loudly as if he was a Canada goose himself.

'Shut your gob, Spike, you sound like one of those rancid riverside geese when you laugh.'

Over on the table, Gus cringed with embarrassment. He hoped his honk didn't sound anything like that.

'Quick, shut up and look sensible,' said Bruce. 'The aromachologist is here.'

TWENTY-SEVEN

THE AROMACHOLOGIST

'Why hellooo, chaps. I'm Mr Eugene Stench, your sniffs and smells expert! You must be Mr Bruce, and you… must be Mr Spike!'

Bruce eyed the vision in front of him suspiciously. He looked like a crazy scientist with wiry hair and round spectacles. On top of his suit was a white laboratory coat. Even weirder was the whiff of girly perfume coming from him.

'I was so intrigued by your phone call last night! Usually when clients come seeking my special talents, they ask for beautiful smells! Just this morning I was working on a new perfume called Eau de Rose Vanilla for Harrods – the Queen's favourite shop, you know the one? But *never* in my long, illustrious, career has anyone called up wanting a smell so foul it makes people roll around in their own vomit! I thought to myself, now *this* is a meeting I must take!'

And *then*, when you suggested The Grand Goose Hotel, well, *of course* I rearranged all my other morning meetings to prioritise you! I've been *dying* to try this hotel; it's just so hard to get a reservation. How on earth did you manage it?'

'Well, I'm a very well-connected businessman,' Bruce lied through his teeth, when actually he'd bribed the young girl on the table reservations team with a couple of the stolen fifty-pound notes.

'Would you like something to eat or drink, Mr Stench?' asked Bruce, praying he wouldn't choose something expensive. He needed some stolen money left to give to Doris for Boris's new school shoes and school dinners. Why couldn't Boris just squeeze his fat feet into last year's shoes and get lunch money for school dinners by stealing it from classmates?

'Oh, I jolly well would, thank you, Mr Bruce. How's about a nice glass of fizz? I do so enjoy a champagne brunch! I'll go for a glass of the Moët & Chandon Dom Perignon Charles & Diana 1961. And to eat, I'll try the Grand Goose signature brunch dish of Lobster Bisque & Scrambled Goose Egg.' Eugene scanned to the bottom of the menu, reading with interest:

The Grand Goose Hotel works with a range of trusted suppliers. We proudly source the finest goose eggs from Cherry Blossom Farm. This is a partnership with Cherry

Blossom's farmer, Abel Greyson, which has
successfully been in place for over a decade.

    Abel Greyson employs the services of
the local 'Goose Whisperer', Siegfried F.
Goosman. Also the proprietor of The Grand
Goose Hotel, Mr Goosman happily divides
his time between ensuring this hotel is
world class, appearing as a guest speaker
at events and advising local farmers on how
to best meet every need of their geese. The
talented Mr Goosman is also a successful
author, having written the acclaimed What
Your Goose Is Thinking. If you would like
to purchase a copy of this outstanding book
for just £49.99, please ask at reception.

Bruce resisted the urge to throttle Eugene, who'd chosen the most expensive items on the menu. For himself, he ordered a 'luxury pork and apple farmhouse sausage sandwich'. His spirits raised a little when Spike said he wasn't hungry and asked for a glass of tap water.

'So,' said Eugene, 'you told me last night all about your company, so I should begin by telling you more about mine. Firstly, though, I must say I absolutely *love* the name of your business. When you said it was called "Fart Fog Security Ltd", I broke out in such hysterical laughter that it took me until I fell asleep to calm down.'

Bruce fixed Eugene with a menacing smile. He didn't like his condescending tone. Failing to notice the fake, snaky aspect of Bruce's smile, he grinned back.

'I've been an aromachologist for many years now and have my own lab just outside West London, where I employ twenty scientists, also known as 'Smell Selection & Creation Experts'. We use smells to create certain emotions in humans. For example, feelings such as relaxation, excitement, happiness and even love… In actual fact, the luxury perfume I'm creating right now has a smell that will make someone fall in love with whoever's wearing it! As I smell of it from working on the fragrance this morning, I wouldn't be surprised if all the ladies and gentlemen in The Grand Goose Hotel are falling in love with me as I speak!'

Bruce snorted unpleasantly.

'Well, as we've already developed a range of smell samples, we've done lots of the hard work for you,' Bruce said. 'I assume this means we get some sort of discount.'

'Sorry, no can do. I'll have to spend time going through all your samples and applying in-depth analysis to them, to determine which smell has the right kind of ghastly effect.'

'Okay, okay.' Bruce scowled. 'Can you please tell me exactly what I'll be getting for my money then, Mr Stench? And when I can expect to get it?'

'Well, first of all, I shall take your bottled fart samples back to the lab. My team and I will don our protective clothing and individually smell each one. We will then all rank them out of ten. Full marks if a sample is *out-of-this-galaxy* puke-inducing. Then, the smells will be run through our state-of-the-art, technically automated analysis machine.'

Bruce had no idea what this was but didn't care to ask and risk looking silly.

'Then, we'll combine all the results, before assigning a rank of awfulness, as I would describe it, to each smell. I'll call in three days' time to confirm the results.'

'And how long will you take to then create the smell in the volume that we require?' queried Bruce, conscious of his timeline.

'My team will then need just a week to do that.'

'Can you cut that to two extra days, and have it all done by Monday? You won't mind working over the weekend, I'm sure!'

'Um, err, yes, I guess so,' he said hesitantly, noticing the snaky element of Bruce's smile this time.

'Excellent!' Bruce exclaimed. He clicked his fingers in the direction of the waitress, summoning her so he could pay the bill. Begrudgingly, he took the stolen gold money clip containing fifty-pound notes out of his pocket. The price of Mr Stench's brunch alone cost the same as a nice holiday on a golden, sandy beach. As he removed the money from the clip, he noticed it had the original owner's name engraved on it in small, fancy writing. Squinting his eyes, Bruce read the name 'Henry Inigo Boniface Wellington-Smythe III'. What a stupid flashy name, he clearly deserved to have his money stolen!

'Why thank you, Mr Stench,' said Bruce, sarcastically. 'We must excuse ourselves now, plenty to be getting on with today!'

'Goodbye, Mr Aroma-Wotsit,' Spike said, holding out his bony arm and hand to shake Eugene's much fleshier one.

*

Just before he left The Grand Hall, Bruce saw that dreadful Betsy woman from his cab relaxing with a large cocktail, topped off with a shiny cherry and paper umbrella. Suddenly, Betsy smelled an enticing aroma of rose and vanilla. Looking over her shoulder, she identified the wearer: a crazy scientist in a pea-green suit and lab coat. He wasn't her usual type, but with a smell so delicious, she felt herself falling in love. She approached Eugene's table to chat him up and see if he wanted to buy her another tropical cocktail. Then, something caught her eye, which made her stop dead.

Next to where he was sitting was another table with various ornaments on, including a stuffed, wild, taxidermy goose! Betsy may have enjoyed wearing hats adorned with birds, but they were *always* fake ones, never real! She was a member of the RSPG, which stood for the Royal Society for the Protection of Geese, and a founding member of the 'Say NO to Fur Club'!

'Nikolaus, Nikolaus,' she called, summoning the head waiter. 'I wish to lodge a complaint IMMEDIATELY! There is a REAL STUFFED GOOSE on that table. It's not right, it's not ethical. Such creatures should have dignity in death!' she erupted, exploding with anger. Her round, fat face had turned puce. 'You must *remove* the offending item at once. Or I shall *never* grace this hotel with my custom ever again!'

Whilst Nikolaus was hurrying over, Betsy Trotter placed her head in her hands and gave little cries of distress, thinking of that poor goose's tragic fate: remaining stuffed forever, while guests around him enjoyed brunch and high tea.

'Madam Trotter, I can assure you that you must be mistaken. This hotel has been owned by a family of goose lovers for centuries. Such an abhorrent item would *never* be displayed here,' Nikolaus said soothingly.

Tentatively, she lifted her face up from her hands. 'But it's over there,' she said, pointing towards the table by Eugene. 'It's… err… err… err…' she stammered, wondering if she was going senile and seeing things. For on the table, there were a few small china goose ornaments. There was absolutely no stuffed, wild goose anywhere in sight.

TWENTY-EIGHT

GOOSE-THEMED HIGH TEA

That stupid, loud art teacher Betsy with the silly hat had rumbled his hiding place! Narrowly avoiding being seen by Nikolaus, Gus dropped to the floor and flattened himself to blend into the goose-print carpet. He needed to get out of The Grand Hall fast! But then what?

Lifting his head just a few millimetres, he spied a potential exit: a door with the word 'Kitchen' written above it in large letters. He slunk flatly towards the door before pushing it open with his beak.

'GO, GO, GO – the first orders for High Tea will be coming in soon, so you IDIOTS had better have all those sandwiches and cakes ready in the next five minutes,' shrieked a man with a badge that said 'ANGELO – HEAD CHEF'. 'Otherwise I'll SACK the lot of you miserable plonkers!'

'ARGH…' Gus stifled a large, angry honk as he felt some silly waitress with a messy, blonde bun step on his tail feather.

'Oh, golly gosh,' she shrieked, stumbling over him, almost sending plates of sandwiches crashing onto his head. He was *not* a happy goose but knew he must keep quiet, carry on and find some way to get out of this hotel! Maybe it would be easier to hide out and rest for a while in the kitchen, which he hoped was a place of peace… *Wrong*!

'DEAN! GET OVER HERE!' Gus heard Angelo screech at a skinny human boy.

'Uh, err, err, uh, yes, Boss?'

'Stop whimpering and simpering like a pathetic mouse. You're a man, for flip's sake! Oh, and fetch today's new printouts of the High Tea menus and put them in their menu stands. But for goodness' sake, DON'T take them out yourself and place them on the tables. Give 'em to Pandora, we wouldn't want to scare the customers with your spotty, pus-ridden mug, would we?'

'Yes, Boss, err, sure,' Dean replied, looking as if he might cry.

Spying a large cooking pot high on a shelf, Gus quietly flew upwards and climbed inside. He poked his head above the rim every so often to get a good look at what was going on. Luckily, the kitchen was a flurry of activity, so no one noticed him.

As Dean began putting the High Tea menus into table stands, Gus poked his head above the cooking pot rim to have a good read. Reading their contents, he felt himself salivating and began hungrily licking his beak.

Goose Themed High Tea
Today's Menu at The Grand Goose Hotel

SAVOURY
Smoked Salmon & Cream Cheese on a Bird-shaped Brioche Roll
18-month aged Comté Cheese in Canada Goose-shaped Soda Bread
Spiced Tomato, Avocado & Emmental on Emden Goose-shaped Bloomer Bre
Feta & Spinach Mini Pies arranged in the shape of a Pomeranian Goose Flo

SWEET
China Goose Cappuccino Cake with a side of Brown Bread Ice Cream
Mongolian Goose Macarons in Mint, Chocolate & Strawberry Flavours
Toulouse Goose Tart with Peach & Apple Jam
Russian Goose Whisky & Dark Chocolate Cake
Sebastopol Goose-shaped Scones with Clotted Cream & Gooseberry Jam

In addition to unlimited amounts of our loose-leaf tea selection, guests may a
choose one of the following cocktails mixed with premium
Grey Goose Vodka

COCKTAILS
Quack-At-Me Cucumber & Elderflower
Feather-Light Lemon
Beaky Berry & Apple

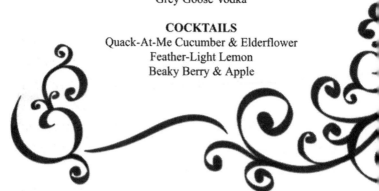

134

Mmmmm… cheese, avocado, spinach, macarons! Gus wasn't exactly sure what *all* these things were, but if that chocolate cake thrown from the taxi window was anything to go by, he'd love it all. And what on earth was a *gooseberry*? Geese couldn't lay berries.

He poked his head out a bit further to get a better look and noticed that the girl who stepped on his tail feather earlier was walking with a limp back into the kitchen.

'Pan-dor-ahhhh! Why so slow, you sill-ly wom-an. Youuuuu arrrrre moooooooving liiiiiike a torrrrrrr-toiiiiiiiiiise!' said Angelo, with a nasty smirk on his face. 'Whyyyyy arrrrrrre youuuuuuu liiiim-pinggggggg?'

Pandora scowled miserably.

'And what on earth is that thing on your head? It looks like a dirty, messy nest. Feral birds could lay eggs in it! Now finish polishing the gold-plated cutlery and then take out the High Tea menus when they're ready.'

Gus was baffled as to why humans chose to work in a kitchen: the one in charge was a ghastly bully! Angelo was right about one thing, though: Pandora's messy bun on top of her head did resemble a bird's nest, and yes, Thomasina could lay an egg containing his offspring in it. Arghhhhh! He put that terrifying thought quickly out of his mind.

Looking down from his cooking pot hideout, he

noticed another pot filled with water beneath him. Another human chef turned something around and suddenly small, blue flames appeared at the base of the pot. They then went orange like normal fire. Gus knew what fire was; he had seen humans having barbecues by the riverside. They always smelt delicious!

To the left of the cooking pot, yet another chef took a freshly baked cake out of an oven. It smelt of Goosey Heaven on earth! He leaned over a little further to get an even better smell…

Feeling the pot teeter on the shelf, Gus panicked and tried to angle it back towards the shelf… but it was precariously balanced, and his attempts were in vain…

For a moment time stood still as disaster loomed…

And then…

CRASH!

Gus shot beak first straight into the pot of water on the cooking hob. The water sizzled as it boiled his flesh alive, before he shot upwards right back out again, piercing the ceiling with his pointy beak whilst letting out a bloodcurdling screech.

The ordeal didn't end there…

On his way down from the ceiling, Gus knocked the pot of boiling water off the hob, catching the edge of his already-trodden-on tail feather in the flames, burning its tip to a black crisp.

Everyone turned simultaneously…

'WHAT WAS THAT ALMIGHTY CRASH?'

'WHY DOES IT SMELL OF BURNT FEATHERS IN HERE?!'

In a complete state of shock, Gus was flying around the kitchen like a crazy goose, unsure of what to do next…

At his maximum speed of seventy miles an hour, he flew so fast he was unidentifiable.

'Oh, for crying out loud,' he heard Angelo shout from what seemed like a million miles away. 'I bet you the hair on my bald head Stupid Steve left the back door to the kitchen open when he went out for his fag break. A feral pigeon must've flown in! Disgusting, diseased birds! Health & Safety will have my head on the chopping block for this!'

Pigeon indeed, thought Gus, annoyed.

'I so did not,' said Stupid Steve.

'Quick, run to close it!' Angelo screeched.

The whole team rushed to the back of the kitchen to check the door, seeing that Steve had indeed shut it.

'I told you, Angelo! So there!' Having finished high school before beginning his chef apprenticeship at The Grand Goose Hotel, Steve was just sixteen years old, rather immature and spoke like a juvenile delinquent. He could work wonders with a kitchen knife, though, often cutting the vegetables into goose shapes for evening dinner, which truly delighted the guests.

After recovering from the initial shock of almost being boiled alive, Gus remembered he needed an escape plan. Thinking quickly, he decided playing dead was his best option. Then Angelo would probably chuck him in the kitchen waste bin. Then, when that was wheeled outside, he would make his escape.

Whilst the team of kitchen staff rushed back into the main kitchen area, on their way back from checking the back door, Gus flew quietly up to the kitchen counter. He lay there hoping someone would discover this 'dead goose' and bin it – instead of cooking and eating it. Relaxing so his wings and webbed feet went floppy, he opened his beak so his tongue lolled out onto the side of the counter.

'I DON'T BELIEEEEVE IT!' Angelo screeched, his voice echoing around the whole hotel. 'The meat supply company has truly screwed up this time! They're meant to supply the poultry already plucked! Now this is going to require loads more work! More time, which we just don't have!

'Steve! Pluck that duck over there! I want it featherless in twenty minutes! When the guests get served their duck à l'orange tonight, they WILL NOT be happy if they see feathers floating around in the orange sauce!'

'Uh, but Angelo, that's not a duck, that's a goose!'

'Can't be, you stupid idiot, I ordered duck meat, not goose meat! Everyone knows The Grand Goose

Hotel has a zero-tolerance policy on serving goose meat. This hotel is a shrine to those bloomin' good-for-nothing creatures. We aren't even allowed to eat their tasty meat!'

'Um, I know you think I'm a bit thick, Boss, but I do know the difference between a duck and a goose. I'm certain that's a goose!'

Angelo looked closer. 'Holy cow, it *is* a flippin' dead goose! If Siegfried F. Goosman finds out there's been a dead goose in the kitchen, he'll sack the lot of us! Quick, Steve, bin that goose immediately! Destroy the evidence.'

Gus felt himself being lifted up by his webbed feet, dangled in the air and then finally dumped in the non-recyclable rubbish bin.

TWENTY-NINE

GOOSE DINNER PARTY

Stepping out into the late afternoon sun, Gus was not a pretty sight. His eyes were bloodshot, he had luminous orange feathers, and he stank of rotting egg and cheese.

During the lunch break, he'd heard Stupid Steve on his phone ordering chicken tikka masala to the hotel staff room. When finished, he discarded the remains of bright orange sauce swimming in greasy oil into the kitchen rubbish bin, where it plopped smoothly on top of Gus's head.

Added to that, his right wing had been resting on mouldy scrambled egg, probably scraped off a plate after brunch. And his left wing had the smelliest cheese known to man smeared all over it. Gus had seen these on the cheese trolley that was offered with biscuits, grapes and chutney after last night's evening meal, including Stinking Bishop, Limburger and Roquefort.

Taking a few tentative steps, he set out along the riverbank to the grassy patch where his family always ate dinner. As he got closer, he was horrified to see Mum had invited not only Grandad but also Thomasina. Normally he loved it when Grandad came to their patch for dinner, but this time, he was just too ashamed for the grandad he idolised to see him in this state. Also, what in the flippin' name of geese was Thomasina doing there? Goose

dinner times were strictly family-only time! Non-family members were only invited when a marriage proposal was imminent... As the penny dropped, Gus almost fainted in horror. His mother was planning on marrying him off to Thomasina!

'Gus, Gus, over here!' Thomasina honked enthusiastically whilst waving her wing zealously.

Drat. Now he had been spotted there was no time to clean himself up before making his grand entrance. If only geese had those wonderful human smartphones! Mum could've texted to warn him about the extra guests. But geese had none of those excellent technical gadgets like humans had: they were dumb and backwards!

He began his descent and waddled the last few metres. Passing the Stecker house, he saw Clara and Boris playing chess on the patio.

'Eww, what is that disgusting smell?' Clara wrinkled her cute little button nose as Gus passed.

'Eurgh, I don't know,' replied Boris, 'but it's much, much worse than even the smell of my dad's farts!'

'Ooh, get your camera out, Cecil,' an old lady said to her husband as they took a riverside walk. 'There's a goose with orange feathers on its head over there! Must be a rare breed; I've never seen anything like it. How very exciting! If you get a good photograph, you might be in with a chance of winning this year's National Geographic Photography Competition!'

'Argh, I don't want to be a model goose with a double-page spread in some silly nature magazine,' Gus hissed to himself. 'I don't want to be a blooming goose at all!' And on that note, he flew the last part of his journey very quickly, thinking he may as well get this tiresome little soirée over and done with.

*

Mum had gone to great efforts for dinner. Each goose sat around the circle with their place mapped out by small green leaves shaping their initials. In the centre was a feast fit for the most important of geese. He saw beans, wheat, grass, corn. But no matter how much effort had gone into scavenging and preparing it, it just wasn't chocolate cake.

Thomasina clapped her wing over her beak trying to stifle her loud honks of laughter. 'Gus, what on earth happened to you?' she said, in between loud, guffawing honks. 'Your head and neck are BRIGHT ORANGE! You look like a CARROT!'

'You know what, Gus? I've had just enough of you and your silly antics lately. I don't even want to know what you've been up to this time!' Mum hissed angrily. 'Now go and clean that stupid head of yours thoroughly, and don't even *think* about coming back until you look respectable enough to sit with us.'

Gus looked away.

'NOW GO!' she shrieked. 'I don't want to see your foolish face again until you can start acting like a mature gander! You're an absolute disgrace to this family! If you carry on, no lady goose is ever going to want to go near you, let alone MARRY you!'

THIRTY

WE NEED TO TALK
ABOUT GUS

Gus took his time getting cleaned up. That cheese and scrambled egg was a nightmare to remove! Every time he dipped his beak into his feathers to fish crumbs out, even more crumbs of cheese revealed themselves. *Oh well,* he mused. Hopefully Mum's little dinner party would be finished by the time he got back.

Waddling tentatively back to the party, he overheard Thomasina make her excuses and leave. Phew.

Then he heard Mum say solemnly to Dad, 'We need to talk about Gus.' Oh man. His parents were about to start one of *those* sorts of chats. Something told him to stay back in the shadows and listen, without showing his face.

'Darling, can it wait until tomorrow, please?' Dad replied. 'It's been a very long and tiring day and I want some sleep.'

'No, I am afraid it absolutely can't.' Mum shot Dad a look that said, 'you dare defy me and I will painfully pluck your feathers out one by one'.

'Okay, okay.'

'Lately, you've been so absorbed with your Prime Goose responsibilities and had your beak completely up in the clouds! So you seem to be oblivious to the fact that our son is having some sort of existential crisis!' Mum hissed.

'You know what goslings are like at Gus's age,' replied Dad. 'All those hormones flying about and finding your place in the flock. It's no biggy.'

Mum turned at Dad, beak square on, whilst letting out a huge honk of exasperation.

'What?' asked Dad. Gus could tell from Dad's expression that he had absolutely *no* idea why Mum had just let out a massive honk in his face. Or why she looked like she was about to cry again. Gus sympathised – he knew what lady geese could be like. They were *very* unpredictable.

'Sorry, darling, what I meant to say is, what *exactly* do you mean by saying "our son is having some existential crisis"? Tell me, darling Goosabella, I'm all ears.'

'Well, I found *this* the other day, I think you should read it,' Mum said, digging up *his* notebook from where she'd re-hidden it.

Noooooo… Mum had his notebook! She knew all about his plan. She knew he wanted to be human. Now Dad was about to know it too. NO NO NO! He wasn't ready for this. He used to think they'd just try and talk him out of it if they knew. But what if it was worse? What if they *actually* tried to ruin his plan and told Grandad he must never introduce Gus to Mr Goosman? Nooo…

'At first, I thought maybe Gus had fallen in with the *bad crowd*, but it is worse, MUCH WORSE!'

'The bad crowd?' asked Dad, looking momentarily confused. 'Who on earth are they?'

'You know… that bunch of hooligan teenage geese that fly around pooing on human heads for a laugh and swiping cigarettes out of mouths before inhaling the smoke through their beaks.'

'Don't be ridiculous, Goosabella!' said Dad. 'Having the Prime Goose's son in their gang would seriously mess up their street cred! I was a cool teenage goose once myself, I know exactly how they roll!'

Dad? Cool?! As. Flipping. If! From his vantage point in the shadows, Gus could now see that Dad was flicking past the first few pages of his notebook to the section that read 'Notes on what humans do – by Gus'. He had a look of mild amusement on his face.

'I have no idea what you find *so* funny here!' hissed Mum.

'You MUST have noticed that Gus has been acting mightily odd lately. Disappearing from your important Annual Goose Meeting, embarrassing us by failing to materialise when you called him up to the podium. Now THAT sure set some beaks wagging. I haven't been able to show my beak at the weekly Lady Goose River Water Drinking Club ever since.'

Mum was staring straight at Dad.

'And you CANNOT have failed to notice that he is hardly ever around these days. He rarely ever shows his face and keeps disappearing off left, right and centre. Now I realise he's a big goose who can look after himself, but a mother goose does have to worry about these things. I know he isn't with Thomasina, Cuthbert and the gang, as every time I ask after him, they tell me they hardly *ever* see him these days. *Oh*, and don't even get me STARTED on his behaviour tonight! All that ridiculous orange gloop on his head and neck… what exactly was *that* about?'

'Shhh, darling, I am trying to finish reading what our son has written,' hissed Dad, sounding frustrated. 'I can't concentrate with your constant loud honking in my ear!'

When Dad finished reading, he let out a huge, honking, snort of laughter, tipping his head back so far that his beak pointed in the opposite direction. 'I think you worry too much, darling wifey.'

'DON'T "*DARLING WIFEY*" ME!'

'He's clearly just going through some crazy phase. Most geese go through a weird phase when they're adolescents. There was a time when I wanted to be an aeroplane. I would watch them wistfully, wishing I had the freedom to fly all over the world. This was, of course, back in the days when our flock didn't migrate. Before I implemented my excellent *Democratic Migration Policy*! It's not as though I actually turned into an aeroplane, though!'

'This is different,' said Goosabella. 'An aeroplane is not a living creature; it wouldn't have been *possible* to become one. A human being, on the other hand, *is* a type of living creature. If Gus tries hard enough, he might actually succeed! Then he'll go and live in a house, get a job, go to human parties and spend the rest of his time staring at one of those small things called smartphones! He would have no time… no time…' Mum's honk was starting to crack now and her eyes welled up with tears again.

'…He would have no time for us *ever* again! Our darling son lost forever to a world of smartphones and large-screen TVs!'

'Darling, think about it rationally,' Dad reassured. 'Our Gus, *live* in a house? Are we even talking about the same goose here? Can you *really* imagine that? He's far too much of a free spirit to be contained by bricks and mortar. As for him getting a job? *Pigs might fly!* I love our son to bits, but if I am entirely honest, he hasn't exactly inherited my fine work ethic! *And* he has the attention span of a goldfish. He's not cut out for the complexity of human life. He would be diving straight back into the River Thames before you could say "Gus is a Goose!"'.

'I'm not so sure,' replied Mum. 'Yes, Gus is a little chilled out and feckless at times, but isn't every goose like that from time to time when they're growing up and finding their webbed feet? I know our son far better than even *he* realises. If there's one thing I'm certain of, it's this: if Gus set his mind on something, he will do everything in his power to achieve it.'

The little appetite Gus had left completely vanished, so he turned away from his parents and swam in the opposite direction. He didn't want to disappoint his mum any further by gracing her with his presence.

THIRTY-ONE

I'M GOING TO
DO IT ALL MYSELF!

'Where've you been, Gus? You didn't come back for dinner. That's not like you.'

'I wasn't in the mood for it, Grandad.' Gus sulked, as he floated a few hundred feet down the riverbank, below The Grand Goose Hotel balconies. He stopped his floating and glumly rested his head in his wings.

'Oh, don't look like that, Gus. It's not so bad. Look – you managed to get out of a romantic meal staged by your mother to make you fall in love with Thomasina. She'll never fancy your feathers again after seeing you with all that orange muck on your head. Now I know she's a lovely young lady goose, but it doesn't take a genius to work out that you don't have romantic feelings for her!'

Gus sighed miserably. 'I just feel like I can't live up to what Mum wants me to be. I know she so desperately wants me married off to Thomasina and to be the next Prime Goose. I get it. She fought hard to be accepted and to get to where she is today: the most important Lady Goose in the flock. I really *do* understand. She thinks just because I'm a teenager, who doesn't talk about my feelings, that I'm a truly heartless lump of feathers. But I'm not! I just can't be what she wants me to be!'

'Okay, Gus, first of all, your mum *does not* think you're a truly heartless lump of feathers. You're very special to her and she loves you very much. Being a mixed-breed goose, she worried she may not be able to hatch her own gosling. Just as your granny also feared she wouldn't be able to; as she was a Chinese goose and me, a Canada goose. In the goose world, nature doesn't always allow different breeds to hatch their own. But both your mum and granny were proven wrong! You really are her miracle son! The day she hatched you was the happiest day of her life!'

'But that's part of the problem! That combined with many other things make me feel the weight of such enormous expectations on my wings! Not only am I her miracle gosling, but our family has fought such discrimination to ultimately triumph in the end. The expectation to carry on the family reputation is like, literally dragging me into the ground!'

'Yes, I can't deny that your mum wants you to be the next Prime Goose and to marry Thomasina, but ultimately, she wants you to be happy. We all do. That's why I want to help you achieve your dream. But… I really do have to be sure that you are mature enough to understand how big a change this would be! And if I'm quite honest, your appearance at dinner tonight didn't exactly scream "mature, grown-up goose"!' Grandad shook his feathers. A few grey ones floated gracefully into the River Thames, contrasting with Gus's silly orange curried ones.

'Oh, there's ALWAYS a reason for you to doubt me, isn't there, *Grandad*! You know, I'm absolutely fed up of all you silly old ancient, bony, geese who think you're so much smarter than I am! You know, forget it, *Grandad*! I'm done with you! I'm done with Mum! I'm certainly done with silly old Dad! But most of all I'm done with your silly little mission, where I must do silly little things to prove to you that I'm serious! I don't need any of you, so bog off! I'M GOING TO DO IT ALL MYSELF!'

THIRTY-TWO

DESIGNER GOOSEBAG

The next morning, after breakfast with his parents, through which he sulked and avoided eye contact, Gus made his excuses and flew off. Everything was going horribly wrong. Mum was still in a hissy mood at him, the pressure to succeed in the Prime Goose election was piling up and to top it all off he'd decided to disown his whole family. Unless they were doing something useful like making his breakfast.

Ways to become human
~~Kiss a human.~~
~~Get Grandad to introduce me to Mr~~
~~Siegfried F. Goosman and ask him to~~
~~transform me into one.~~
Get one of the people at the school to
make me human as part of the Goose
Virtual Reality Goggles project?!

It's not as if kissing one worked, and now he'd cancelled Grandad, the Mr Goosman plan certainly wouldn't happen. This basically left one option. Ugh.

He'd have to go to that school again. Hmm. There was still a problem. He didn't care about impressing silly old Grandad, but he still wanted to stop the Bacon burglary! After all, Clara was his Human Mummy and she needed to know! BINGO – he had an idea. He'd kill two birds with one stone (what a ghastly phrase!) and go to school to achieve two goals. Not *only* could he decide on who to transform him into a human, but he could also have a nice little honk with Clara and warn her about Bruce Bacon and his evil plan!

Gus flew to school and settled in a corner of the playground to do some final work. Now his masterplan was concluding, he needed to give great thought to exactly what type of human he'd be. Admiring the park's beautiful scenery, Gus sat, notebook in front of him, pen poised in beak. The other day he'd neatly reburied it after Mum tossed it aside in rage. With great care, he began adding the finishing touches to his plan…

My Human Life Plan — by Gus

Step 1: Get job. Not sure what this will be yet, but it CERTAINLY won't be a teacher. That looks way too stressful and like lots of hard work and the human children don't even listen to you!

Step 2: Get house. My house will have stylish furniture and always be tidy. Unlike Bruce and Spike's hovel of a flat, where you can barely see anything because of all the dirty pots, pans and clothes strewn everywhere. I am hoping I can afford to buy a lovely house on the river like the Steckers. Then it will be nice and convenient for my family and friends to come round for a human-style dinner party, where we'll eat at a table!!!

Step 3: Buy fashionable human clothes...

Just as he was putting his finishing touches to the plan, a human girl spied him in his corner and sashayed towards him, flicking her long, blonde hair. *'This one looks like a friendly dude, he'll do!'* she squealed. Before he had time to hiss, honk, flap his wings or protest, he felt her brightly painted fingernails scoop him up and bundle him into her super-large designer handbag. Then he felt himself bounce up and down in her fancy handbag as she skipped off.

Argh – what was happening? Who was this girl? She looked much too big to be a school child and her bag was nothing like Clara's! Maybe she wasn't a school human at all! Terrifying thoughts reeled through his head. Maybe she'd pluck out his feathers one by one and stuff her silk pillows with them? Maybe she was a chef and he'd be on the specials board in a fancy restaurant that evening? Oh, heavens on earth! There would be nothing left of him! His poor family, they would be grief-stricken, never knowing what had become of him…

He looked around the handbag to find an escape…

Suddenly the terrifying thoughts floated away as he noticed his luxurious surroundings… The inside of the human's bag was quilted with a very fancy lining. Gus rubbed his head feathers against it, enjoying the comfort of soft, warm fabric. Ooooh… and what was that? He saw a beautiful gold and black glass bottle emblazoned with the words 'Giorgio Armani – Rose D'Arabie'. He pulled the bottle top off and sprayed a few squirts on his feathers. Geese might not be able to smell, but he liked the idea of other humans finding him fragrant.

Further rummaging unveiled many other treasures. A small, glittery zip bag revealed various items of makeup. He'd been spying on humans long enough to know what makeup was! Holding the small vanity mirror in his wing, he applied bright red lipstick to his beak and dusted his cheek feathers with blusher.

*

After picking up a decaffeinated soy skinny latte, the human finally arrived at her desk. She opened her bag, hauled Gus out by the feel and plonked him right by the side of a painting easel. Hanging her handbag on his beak like he was some kind of coat hook, she flashed a smile of pearly white teeth.

'Darling goosey – hi! I'm Emma Louise Wellington, nice to meet you. Please be good. Otherwise, I won't be able to bring you to GCSE art class again, and I think you and I could be BFFs forever!'

GCSE art class?

'Yep,' she shrieked excitedly, as if registering his confusion. 'Mrs Trotter emailed my mum to say we're painting what we think a goose would see! For some dumb old techy goggle thingies! What a bore! And... that we could bring in a super cute real-life goosey like you to use as a life drawing model! Cause I guess a goose would see lots of other geese on the river! So, I'll paint a few of you!'

Looking around, he saw other children had brought in bits of grass and mud to paint.

'Yoohoo! Gus! Gus! Psst! Over here!' came a familiar honk. 'Oh, isn't this *wonderful*! I always thought I had model potential.'

'What are *you* doing, here, Thomasina?' Gus hissed, almost fainting with shock at seeing another goose in a human classroom... and why did it have to be HER?

'Well, I was just, you know, stretching my fabulous feathers with the girl goose gang earlier and looking divine on my morning swim, and this human girl here OBVIOUSLY chose me as the prettiest goose of all to take to school to paint! Wonderful, isn't it? Maybe we could model as a couple and get someone to paint us as we kiss!'

Gus shuddered.

'Ooh, is that lipstick you're wearing, Gus? Where did you get it? Gimme gimme gimme!'

At that moment Mrs Trotter came click-clacking into the classroom in her high heels, followed by Sarah Stecker, who was wearing a much more sensible pair.

'WHAT ON EARTH IS GOING ON IN HERE!' said Mrs Trotter. 'Arghh! What are those two birds doing in my art room?' She screeched and climbed onto the top of the art supplies cupboard quivering with fear.

'Uh, well – you did email our parents on Monday telling us to bring in riverside things to paint, like mud, grass or a goose,' said a girl who was painting what was actually a very good riverside scene with Thomasina swimming in it.

'I was JOKING about the goose bit, Sophie!' screeched Mrs Trotter at the poor girl. 'What *are* your parents, stupid or something? Actually, don't answer that! Your parents clearly didn't get the joke either, did they, Emma! And what on earth is the kind of goose you've brought in? It has a red beak and pink cheek feathers!'

'I thought you loved geese, miss! You said the other week you're a member of the RSPG!'

'That doesn't mean I want feral ones in my classroom, Emma!'

'Mrs Trotter?' chimed in Sarah Stecker. 'I've got the VR goggles today for the children to try. You know, like I said I would bring them in? Why don't you come down and try them?'

'Argh, no, I'm staying right up here until those feathered things leave my art class!'

'Never mind,' said Sarah, who looked completely at ease in a small classroom with him and Thomasina present. 'How about you try them?' Sarah asked, smiling at Emma Louise Wellington.

'Ooh yeah!' Emma Louise shrieked, before leaping out of her chair with excitement. She skipped to the front of the classroom and took the goggles. Gus watched intently, trying to distract himself from a poo he was desperate to do. This was the moment of truth! When Emma tried on the goggles, she'd miraculously turn into a goose. Proof that the goggles could make someone change species!

'Enjoy pretending to be a goose.' Sarah smiled, as Emma-Louise put them on.

Pretend to be a goose? Pretend? PRETEND?!

Gus felt his feathers shake. It was as if someone had punched him. Tears formed in the corner of his eyes. This was the most tragic news EVER! Maybe Grandad was right. Maybe Mum was right. He was a stupid immature goose after all. So stupid and immature that he'd misunderstood in a fit of excitement when he first visited the school. After all the clue was in the name – 'Virtual Reality' goggles. Virtual isn't real. The glasses couldn't make children into geese! They could only let them pretend!

Emma placed the goggles on her head. The final proof was there: she didn't change species...

If the bird experience was not about turning humans into *real* birds but instead simulating the experience, even the smartest person at the school was unable to do the reverse of this transformation: turn a goose into a human. He was all out of options and would remain a ghastly, awful, boring old goose FOREVER.

THIRTY-THREE

THE WORST GOOSE EVER

Gus sat flicking through his extended notes on Mission: Human. He'd worked SO hard. But it was all pointless, because he'd been horrid to his loving grandad, who certainly wasn't going to be interested in having anything to do with his mean grandson now. He'd even forgotten to try and warn Clara about the burglary as he was so caught up in his own selfish desires. That, and he'd needed to get out and do his poo. He'd suffered from a condition called IBS (Irritable Bird Syndrome) for years, which meant when you gotta go, you gotta go. So, holding it in had been painful. But still. It was official. He was the WORST. GOOSE. EVER.

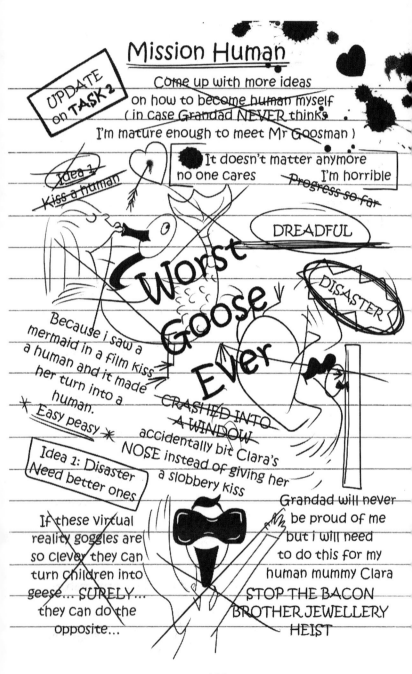

Mission Human

Come up with more ideas on how to become human myself (in case Grandad NEVER thinks I'm mature enough to meet Mr Goosman)

~~Idea 1~~
~~Kiss a human~~

It doesn't matter anymore no one cares

I'm horrible

~~Progress so far~~

DREADFUL

Worst Goose Ever

DISASTER

Because i saw a mermaid in a film kiss a human and it made her turn into a human.

★ Easy peasy ★

~~CRASHED INTO A WINDOW~~ accidentally bit Clara's NOSE instead of giving her a slobbery kiss

Idea 1: Disaster Need better ones

If these virtual reality goggles are so clever they can turn children into geese... SURELY... they can do the opposite...

Grandad will never be proud of me but i will need to do this for my human mummy Clara

STOP THE BACON BROTHER JEWELLERY HEIST

'Gus, Gus,' came a familiar and reassuring honk from the distance. 'Come on, let's kiss and make up. I know you didn't mean what you said yesterday and you're just frustrated with life.'

'But I'm horrible! I don't deserve you!' Gus hissed back, as Grandad swooped down beside him. 'I'm the WORST GOOSE EVER!'

'Don't be so dramatic – no, you're not! Just try and think before you honk out hurtful words next time, if that's okay with you.'

'I promise, Grandad.' Gus smiled, before planting a sticky kiss on his beak.

'What's this then? I thought you were much too grownup to kiss your ancient family members!'

'Maybe I'm not so smart after all, Grandad.'

'Rubbish, what's happened to my cocky arrogant grandson? And what's this that you're writing?'

'Oh, it's my Human Plan,' said Gus, indiscreetly biting out the pages that contained the note about the Bacon burglary before sitting on them. Grandad absolutely couldn't find out about this part until Gus had succeeded! He might fear for his safety and try and stop him! Then he'd never get to prove what a smart hero he was and meet Mr Goosman.

'What on earth are you doing, Gus? Why are you eating your Human Plan?'

'I'm not eating it, silly! I'm making a comfortable seat out of it! I hate sitting on dry grass!'

'You are a funny old goose sometimes! Whoever

heard of a goose that was too precious to sit on grass!' Grandad cackled. 'Anyway, show me the rest!'

Gus nervously handed over the notes on his human life plan, about what kind of job and house he might like. Smiling, Grandad had a flick through.

'You know what, maybe I've been too hard on you. You have been giving this some serious thought, haven't you?'

'Uh huh.'

'Well, maybe… just maybe… I could introduce you to Mr Goosman. As long as you promise not to turn up with orange feathers!'

'Oh! Would you? Would you really, Grandad?'

'I suppose I could.' Grandad smiled.

'YIPPEEEEE! Oh I promise you won't regret it, I promise, promise, promise! But first of all, there is something else I need to focus on!'

For once, it was time to put someone else before him. He would rescue his Human Mummy Clara and the Steckers from the evil Bacons and their plans to steal their beautiful jewels. He just needed to come up with a good plan… With a further renewed sense of motivation, Gus flew off excitedly, as Grandad looked on, baffled.

THIRTY-FOUR

SMELLY NEWS

BRINNNNG BRINNNNNG, BRINNNNG
BRINNNNNG…

Bruce awoke to a ghastly sound with a terrible
headache, self-inflicted from too many beers the
night before. He stood up, put on his grease-stained
dressing gown and stumbled across to the phone,
almost tripping over empty beer cans and falling flat
on his face.

'Wuh huh?' he answered, half asleep and with
greasy morsels from yesterday's midnight snack
wedged between his teeth.

'Hello, Mr Bacon! It's your aromachologist here.'

Ah yes, that nasty little stench, Eugene. Bruce
jolted himself awake to concentrate. Today was the
day that he would hear the result of Eugene's smell
analysis on his bottled farts.

'Oh, hello, Mr Stench,' Bruce replied with fake

charm. As far as he was concerned, Eugene could take his pea-green suit and fancy university degrees and shove them up his bum. But then again, Google had told him that Eugene Stench was the best smell expert in the country, so he needed his expertise to pull off his super plan.

'Aww, you sound a little worse for wear, Mr Bacon! Few too many lagers with the lads last night?'

Bruce made rude gestures with his fingers down the phone. How dare Eugene judge him for doing something normal like drinking forty cans of beer on a midweek night!

'So, let's get to it then,' continued Eugene, 'the news you have been waiting for... After an in-depth analysis using our super smell-ometer, invented by yours truly, of course, the result was unanimous! That *fried sausage* fart of yours was truly off the scale! Now when a copy of *that* smell is produced on an industrial scale, any wannabe thief shall wish he'd never been born!'

Bruce chuckled to himself under his breath.

'But I must warn you: there is a minor operational hitch! Most of my team of Smell Selection & Creation Experts are extremely poorly and off work. Whilst carrying out the subjective analysis by smelling your farts themselves, they started to feel ill and have been projectile-vomiting on and off ever since. The worst case is a young chap named Brian, bless him. He's been puking so much he's literally lost half his body weight! His doctor's put him on a medically advised high-calorie diet of burgers, chips and fried Mars Bars to get back up to his normal weight and strength. All down to the potency of your *fried sausage* fart sample!'

'Fear not, though, I might add!' Eugene said in jolly tones. 'I'm absolutely fine as I don't work on the day-to-day activities like doing the smelling. I just lead the team and motivate them! No need for me to get involved in the nitty-gritty of a smelly task like this!'

'Oh, and we also have two other team members who are still bright and breezy! Jock and Stevo – just their nicknames, I might add! – could handle it. They play rugby at weekends, so they can handle all sorts of unpleasant smells after all those foul drinking games and puking antics they get up to as rugby lads!'

Bruce chortled. Eugene Stench was a try-hard who liked to think he was 'down with the kids' by using words like 'lads' and referring to people by their silly nicknames. If he'd been in Bruce's class at school, Bruce would have jammed a fart bottle so far up his elephant ear-like nostrils that it would have pierced through the top of his head.

'So, what does this mean for me then, this smaller team size?' Bruce hissed.

'Well, unfortunately there's going to be a small additional charge as Jock and Stevo will have to work *very* hard under my supervision this weekend.'

'Okay,' Bruce said, annoyed, hoping he'd be long gone and relaxing on a sunny beach by the time Eugene's invoices came through. 'I'll meet you at your laboratory on Monday to collect the first batch of *fried sausage* Fart Smell. Have it well sealed in something airtight, by the way.'

'Will do, Mr Bruce. Give my love to Mr Spike. Ta-ta for now!'

Bruce slammed down the phone.

*

'Ooh what was that then, Bruv? I heard someone say give love to Mr Spike! Was it one of 'em gorgeous women that you always chat about, that fancies you? The ones I've never met? Oooh – she must've seen my gorgeous self when out and about with you!' Spike smiled, raised his eyebrow and flexed his spaghetti-string arms.

'DON'T BE SO RIDICULOUS! No lady would even touch you with a pooey stick!' screeched Bruce.

'Oh, I guess not, Bruv,' Spike replied, looking like he was about to cry. 'They all want to date just you, cause you is so gorgeous!'

'Anyway, come over here, you lazy oaf,' Bruce said, softening his tone a little to stop Spike locking himself in the loo to cry and becoming even more useless than he already was. 'I've been doing all the difficult brain work by myself and it's about time you made yourself useful! We've got our first meeting at Tom Stecker Jewellery this afternoon – our system must be in tip top shape.'

'Oh, sorry, Bruv. It's just that you is so good at all them brainy bits. Poor old simple me doesn't 'alf get confused! Figured it was best to let the brains get on wiv it! We're like Beauty and the Brains, us, I'll just sit and look dead 'andsome when we go and meet that lady who owns the jewellery shop and you do all the talking!'

Bruce made a guffawing sound.

'HOW MANY TIMES DO I HAVE TO TELL YOU IT'S A GEEZER THAT OWNS THE JEWELLERY SHOP! And anyway, it's called TOM STECKER JEWELLERY! Does *Tom* sound like a lady?'

'Uh… guess not, Bruv,' Spike replied after much deliberation with himself.

'Okay, I'll run through the various components that I've cleverly built and tell you what we need to do. Now this, on the right-hand side of the table here, is what's known as the *alarm*. This is the part we install on the shop wall. Listen carefully: the way this works is by detecting something called *infrared radiation*.'

'Infa-wotsit?'

'For the purposes of your minuscule little brain, just think of it as heat that comes from someone walking by or, say, smashing something with an axe! When there's a sudden increase in this heat, an alarm is triggered.'

'You get so 'ot and sweaty just walking from the couch to the toilet as you is so fat, Bruv, I is surprised you ain't triggering off alarms everywhere!' Spike honked with laughter like a long, thin, bony goose.

'Shut that hole in yer face and put the alarm component into that smart, black cardboard box. I made that to transport it to the shop in. If we're going to look professional, we need fancy packaging for our system.'

'Okay, Bruv,' replied Spike, immediately doing as he was told.

'And this here... now this is the REAL masterpiece,' Bruce said proudly, pointing to a canister fixed to the alarm. 'This will contain large quantities of the chemicals that make up the copycat version of my *fried sausage fart*. On Monday, I'll go and collect the first batch of smell from that posh git Mr Stench. Then, it'll be pumped into this gruesome green canister ready for use, when some jewel thieves enter the jewellery shop!' said Bruce, chuckling evilly.

Spike nodded dumbly.

'Now put the canister into that big black box over there.

'Now, we need to explain all of this to Tom! But unbeknownst to him, we are COMPLETELY immune to my gorgeous fried-sausage farts! Ahh, we smell them so often we won't get ill and puke up whilst falling ill to the floor! We could even eat them on toast or bathe in them in a bubble bath! Anyway, you get the idea! Whilst everyone else is writhing sick on the floor, this will give us both a chance to grab the valuable jewels, run out of the shop, skedaddle to the airport and go to a well-hidden location with pretty girls and sandy beaches!

'But, best of all, *this time* there will be absolutely no FLIPPIN' GOOSE TO RUIN OUR MASTERPLAN!'

THIRTY-FIVE

JEWELLERY SHOP

'Spike – you carry the boxes containing the security system. We'll show it all to Tom and impress him! But, for goodness' sake – DON'T YOU DARE OPEN YOUR MOUTH AND SPEAK! We want this meeting to be a success! If you so much as utter one word, just one measly word, we're screwed! So just shut up, yeah? Got that into your thick head?'

'Yeah, Bruv. I don't really fancy talking in a business meeting anyway. Requires too much brain work, if ya get what I mean!' Gus heard Spike reply, as he tailgated them all the way from Putney riverside to the Tom Stecker Jewellery shop.

Waddling inconspicuously behind them, Gus thought how ridiculous the pair of them looked. Bruce's gut was in a constant fight with his suit jacket to break free, whereas Spike's looked as if a whole other man could fit in it. He slunk in behind Bruce who led the trio stoutly into the shop, looking as if all his Christmases had come once. Hot on Gus's webbed feet was Spike, who, on entering the shop, immediately tripped over him and fell face-first. Boxes of the new security system spilled their contents all around him.

'HONNNNNNNNNKKKKKKK!' screeched Gus as a heavy, black box fell right on top of him, squashing him flat.

The sound of the falling box and Tom worriedly hurrying towards Spike to help him up drowned out Gus's bloodcurdling honk. Lying to his right, Gus noticed plenty of loose black fabric. After plumping himself back up into the shape of a living, breathing goose, instead of something from the Sainsbury's refrigerator section, he crawled into this black fabric to hide.

Peeking from underneath it, he saw an array of the most *beautiful* stones he had ever seen – human children didn't throw stones like that into the River Thames! His favourite was a pair of earrings labelled 'Dangling Alexandrite'. They swished and sparkled elegantly on their stand, shifting from petal-pink through to stunning cerise all the way to gorgeous green. Next to the stand it said '£1 million', but Gus had no idea whether this was a lot of money or not for a pair of earrings. Then he saw Bruce salivating like a dog in a meat factory.

'Mr Bacon, please, let me help you up,' Gus overheard Tom say to Spike.

'Oh, my precious darling brother,' cooed Bruce, summoning fake tears to his eyes. 'Are you alright? I'm SOOO worried about you! Whatever would I do without you, my precious flesh and blood! Please let me help you up, too! Tom – do you have a nice, comfortable chair for my dear, injured brother to rest in?'

Eurgh, gimme a break, thought Gus, rolling his eyes in disbelief under the shroud of black material.

'Yes, yes, of course,' said Tom, pointing to a fancy chaise longue positioned by the wall of the shop to add to its glamorous atmosphere. 'You can rest there.'

As Tom and Bruce helped Spike to his feet, Gus realised what he was hiding in. As the fabric began to move, Gus felt himself slip into view. Panicking, he quickly gripped on to Spike's shirt with his flight feathers as Spike rose to his feet.

'Clara, Clara – can you make my guest a nice cup of sugary tea, please? He's just had a nasty fall and feels very faint!'

'Sure, Daddy,' came that sweet, familiar little voice from out back. *My Human Mummy! What a lovely surprise, I didn't expect her to be here!*

'I hope you don't mind – my daughter Clara's helping me out here as it's teacher-training day at school today. I should've told you actually, I know she likes playing with your son!'

'*The fat little toad's with his mother today,*' Bruce hissed under his breath.

'What was that, Mr Bacon? Sorry, I didn't catch what you said,' replied Tom.

'Oh, I said, the sweet little darling's with his mother today,' Bruce said, laying the charm on thick.

'There you go, Mister Bacon.' Clara smiled, handing Spike his cup of tea. 'Are you feeling any better now?' she asked, looking strangely at Spike's 'large' stomach.

'Uh, yeah,' said Spike, 'although me chest and stomach feel much heavier than they usually do.'

'Daddy… I'm getting a bit bored here. There's nothing to do,' Gus heard Clara whine.

'Clara, please be quiet, I'm trying to have a business meeting,' Tom replied.

'But Daddy, I don't trust these men! Boris is always saying how naughty his dad is! And why has Boris's skinny Uncle Spike got a stomach like a pregnant lady?'

'Clara – shhhh. You mustn't say such things, it's not polite! I'll tell you what, here's a couple of pounds – why don't you pop to the sweet shop next door and get something whilst we have our boring grownup business meeting!'

'Oh-kaaaaay. But Daddy, I think you should be, like, really careful! These men look just like the baddies from *Home Alone* – and they're big trouble!'

Gus hastily abseiled down Spike's leg and revealed himself from underneath his hiding place. Luckily no one noticed. He'd been given another BIG CHANCE – he could get his Human Mummy on her own and try very hard to get her to understand his goose honks. She was VERY smart – maybe, just maybe, if he tried hard enough it would work, and he could warn her about the Bacons' wicked plan!

THIRTY-SIX

SWEET SHOP

'OH MY GOSH, IT'S YOU AGAIN! My little feathered friend!' Clara squealed.

'HONK HONK HONK HONK HONK HONK HONK!'

'Why are you looking so sad? I thought you wanted to be friends?'

'Honk. Honk. Hissety. Honk.' Gus thumped his webbed foot on the shop floor.

'You're a funny one, goose. Anyway, it was hilarious in art class the other day, Barry was absolutely terrified of you, and normally he's the one scaring everyone at school!' Clara giggled.

'HISSSSSSSSSSSSSSSSS.'

'So what are you up to this time? I didn't know geese like sweets! Aren't you meant to eat mud and grass? And why are you always following me?'

'HONKKKKKKKKKKKKKKKKKKKKK!'

'Are you trying to tell me something? Please stop bashing your beak on that shop wall – you'll hurt yourself!'

'HONK HISSSSSSSSSS!'

'I'm so sorry, I don't understand! I wish we could, but humans can't speak "goose"!'

'HISSSSSSSSSSSSSSSSSSSSSSSSSSSSSSSSSSSSSS! Munch. Munch!'

'Why are you licking my jumper? Oooh, I know! You're hungry!' Clara rummaged in her pink glittery unicorn rucksack and took out a brown paper bag.

Gus looked at Clara with disgust.

'Don't look so cross – look! It's leftover bird seed from when Boris and I went to the park to feed the ducks after school the other day! Here you go, goose!'

Clara smiled and handed Gus some dry seeds from the brown bag she was offering. He promptly spat it out all over her jumper.

'How rude! Oh well, suit yourself! I'm hungry so *I'm* going to choose my sweets, even if you don't want your treat.' Clara selected a sherbet dip, some chocolate buttons and some jelly babies, before putting them into the pink and white striped bag on the pick and mix sweet counter.

'Clara?'

'Yes, Mrs Benson,' Clara said to the sweet-shop lady.

'Look, I know you're normally a really well-behaved girl and you've been coming to my shop for years with your dad, but can you *please* not bring a wild animal in ever again! It's scaring off all the other customers!'

Once safely out of the shop, Gus raised his beak and snatched the pink and white striped paper sweet bag.

'Oi, that's mine,' shrieked Clara. 'Gimme it back! Give it BACK!'

Clara tried to grab the bag back and a tug-of-war ensued.

'HONK!'

'GIVE IT BACK.'

'Hisssssss!'

'Oi, goose! It's mine! I tried to give you some tasty bird seed but you didn't want it. NOW. GIVE. ME. THE. SWEETS. BACK.'

Gus gave one final tug and succeeded in wrangling the sweets from Clara's little hand, before flying off into the distance, chomping on jelly babies and slobbering sweet juice as he went.

'Clara – get in the shop,' Tom shouted, opening his shop door. 'What on earth is all that commotion outside!' He looked down at her empty hands.

'I can't believe you've scoffed all those sweets already. You'll be sick.'

'I promise I didn't, Daddy! A goose won tug-of-war and ate them,' Clara wailed.

'Look, I know you didn't want to come into work with me today and just wanted to play at home, but that's no reason to make up such silly stories! Now behave for the rest of the afternoon, please. Or no pocket money!'

*

'I must say, it's a truly unique system and definitely one I want to try in future,' Tom said, turning his attention back to the Bacons as Clara sulked in the staff kitchen at the back of the shop. 'But we haven't had our current security system installed for very long and I think it's a good one,' Tom said, as he flicked through the glossy sales brochure for Fart Fog, created on Bruce's stolen Apple computer the night before.

'Ah, but you never know where the next dangerous thief is lurking!' Bruce said ironically. 'And with your current system, yes, it's true the thick smoke will prevent the thief from getting to the jewels as they won't be able to see them. But, and this is a *big* but, the thief will still easily be able to turn around, run out of your shop and escape down Hatton Garden before making a quick getaway on the tube train. Probably fly off to some sunny beach somewhere. However… with our excellent Fart Fog system, the thief will be too busy puking his guts up on the floor from the foul-smelling fog. Then ta-dah! The police will zoom in and capture him! And you must be *so* careful these days. There've been so many heists in recent years, *especially* that really big one that happened two years ago!'

'Hmmm, true,' said Tom, looking thoughtful.

'You know what, Mr Stecker, how about I give you a FREE three-month trial period? If you're still not convinced, you can easily go back to your current system, no problem!' Bruce replied, on a roll.

'Oh, go on then.'

'Great!' said Bruce. 'How about I come in with the contract on Monday afternoon for you to sign? We can even install it then!'

'Why not?' said Tom. 'Have a lovely evening, both! I look forward to your wonderful Fart Fog system keeping my shop safe from all the naughty burglars out there!'

THIRTY-SEVEN

A PLAN UNFOLDS

'Oh, Spikey, Spikey, tra-la-la!' Bruce sang in an uncharacteristically friendly tone as he leapt out of bed the next morning. 'Our days in this smelly dump of a flat are finally numbered, my dearest Spikey!'

From the other side of the windowpane Gus snorted in disbelief. The only reason the flat smelt was because Bruce was constantly farting and never tidied up his dirty plates.

'Yep,' he continued, 'this time next week, we'll be lying on a sandy beach with a pretty lady in a nice bikini giving us back massages and fruity cocktails!'

'What's that noise, Bruv?' Spike asked, cocking his ear towards the window.

'What on earth are you talking about? It's probably in that stupid, idiotic head of yours!' Bruce snapped, his pleasant mood fast evaporating.

'No, Bruv, I is serious. It sounds like something is snorting at the window. But it don't sound like an oinky, piggy type of snort. It sounds like a birdy-snort from one of 'em gooses.'

'Don't be so thick. A bird wouldn't snort, only pigs do. Flippin' hell, did you learn nothing at school? Now let me explain the plan to you. The next few days are very important and I need you to know exactly what's going on!'

'Now take a look at this!' Bruce said proudly, thrusting a large piece of paper under Spike's nose. On the paper were a load of strange shapes and arrows.

'What on earth is this then, Bruv? I has never seen anyfink like it!' Spike scrutinised the contents of the piece of paper.

'It's a diagram of the shop floor of Tom Stecker Jewellery, you bony, old dimwit!'

From where he was perched, Gus saw the so-called 'diagram'. He was with Spike on this one. It didn't remotely resemble what it was meant to. Instead, it looked like scribblings from a fat wax crayon, drawn by one of those chubby human toddlers he saw out and about down Putney High Street in chairs on wheels. Bruce snatched the diagram back off him angrily and laid it out on the only floor space he was able to find in the lounge, which was a task in itself.

'Now concentrate!' he snapped at Spike.

Gus tried to concentrate too, but it was hard when he felt so sick after stuffing all Clara's sweets down his beak yesterday. Snatching them off her was mean, but he just couldn't help himself, and he needed to cheer himself up after failing so spectacularly at warning her about the plan. As hard as he tried, he just couldn't get her to understand his hisses and honks.

'Er, Bruv?'

'WHAT NOW?'

'I just heard another strange noise,' said Spike, cocking his ear to the window again. 'It sounds like some riverside goose retching after eating too many sweeties or something.'

Bruce slammed his fist in the table in anger. 'DON'T BE SO BRAIN-DEAD! GEESE DON'T EAT SWEETS, YOU DIMWIT! Now for the millionth time, concentrate. This here is the door to the shop. And this rectangle shape here is the window display – called the win-dow dis-play be-cause it is in frrr-ont offf thhhhhe winnnnn-dowwwwwwwww,' Bruce explained, purposely slowing down his syllables to make it easier for Spike to follow.

'This bit here, as you can see, because of how it's shaped, is the chaise longue that you rested on whilst clever-clogs me was doing all the hard work and successfully running the business meeting. See, in front of it, you can also see the table and the other fancy chairs. I can imagine this is where Mr Stecker himself sits with his *fancy* clients, talking to them about his *fancy* jewellery, whilst offering them a *fancy* cup of loose-leaf tea in bone china or something stupid like that,' said Bruce sneeringly.

Bruce gave an evil laugh and smirked before continuing. 'But, unbeknown to him at this moment, Mr Smug Successful Jewellery Shop Owner will have none of his fancy, flashy jewellery to sell in just a few short days' time!'

Gus pressed his beak down as flat as possible so that it was parallel to the windowpane and his eyes were closer, peering beadily in. He wanted to get a better look at the diagram for comedy value. When he succeeded, he stifled a huge, honking laugh at what he saw. Bruce's table and chairs were the funniest-looking table and chairs he had ever seen. Then there were the stick men behind the glass counter display. A monkey could've drawn it better.

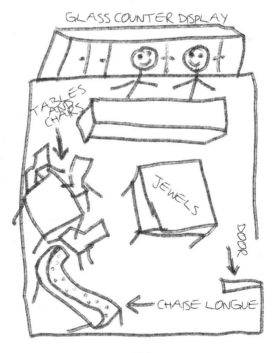

'Against the back wall of the shop are the pedestal glass displays. Behind them are wall-mounted glass cabinets.'

'Uh huh, Bruv,' said Spike, peering at the diagram with a perplexed look on his face.

'Now, Spike, the next things I need to tell you are the most important, so concentrate that stupid brain of yours and listen!'

'As we walk into the shop,' he continued, 'you will remember seeing to the right of us a large, glass counter display that runs almost the full length of the shop wall. Behind it is where whoever is on duty that day will be standing, ready to unlock the counter and take out whatever it is the customer wants to see in more detail.'

Spike scratched his head, and then his backside for good measure, trying to summon up the memory of this display in his mind.

'Now I have thought long and hard about this, and decided we are going to do a "Smash and Grab" robbery. This means that we go in carrying axes, dressed in black burglar masks to disguise us. Then, we smash the display counter, swipe everything and make our escape.'

Spike nodded at Bruce, mouth slightly ajar.

'Once we run out of the shop, we will skedaddle into one of the nearby alleyways. There, we will quickly change into our smart casual clothes and get a cab to the airport, where we check in for our flights.'

'So where is it that we is escapin' to?' asked Spike, drooling with excitement like a dog with a juicy bone.

'Now this is where clever-clogs me has come up trumps again!' said Bruce, whipping out a couple of travel tickets from his back pocket and waving them in front of Spike's face.

'Dub... Dub... Dubah... Dub-wotsit?'

'For crying out loud, it says DUBAI!' said Bruce exasperatedly. 'It's where we are escaping to once we have stolen the jewellery! Great place: very hot, sandy beaches, lots of expensive things to buy like flashy cars and all that... AND... Best of all... even if we get identified as the jewellery thieves, the authorities in Dubai will not be sending us back to England to be put in prison!'

'Genius, Bruv!' said Spike enthusiastically.

'I even have the phone numbers of a couple of fences from my days doing the odd job for Mad Dog O'Banion. You know the one – he scared you so much you practically peed your pants every time he came around.'

Spike shuddered at the mention of Bruce's old accomplice.

'So, we can swap the jewellery for cold, hard cash as soon as possible,' said Bruce, with a glint in his eye.

'Err, why would a fence have a phone?' asked Spike. 'I remember that white fence that Grandma had when we was little. The one you used to draw rude fings and other graffiti on. How on earth can you talk to a fence on a phone? It ain't a real, speaking fing, Bruv!'

Bruce sighed with frustration and rested his face in his fat, greasy palms. 'NOT THAT TYPE OF FENCE,' he screeched. Then, worrying their neighbour might hear what they were up to, he lowered his voice. 'A *fence* is a criminal who buys stolen goods from thieves and sells them on. The sooner we can exchange the jewellery for cash the better – cash can't be traced. We need the fences because it takes a *great* amount of time and effort selling stolen goods. Time I won't have when I am too busy driving my own customised Ferrari. Besides, I need a rest from all this hard work! It's not as if you've been pulling your weight when it comes to our business ventures and criminal activity. You're flippin' lucky to have me as a brother!'

Spike nodded and smiled, looking unsure.

'Now, let's take a break before dinner and go through the finalised plan this evening.'

THIRTY-EIGHT

GUS PREPARES FOR THE BIG DAY

Gus awoke feeling groggy with a dull headache. The searing sun shone through gaps in the tree branches, telling him it was getting late. Drat. He'd massively overslept. Rolling out of his riverside bed, he felt around for his trusty notebook. Waves of nausea rolled over him as he remembered the night before, watching through the Bacons' flat window while Bruce ate fifteen fat sausages, followed by a pack of pork scratchings, then a supersize family bag of Walkers Pork Pie flavour crisps.

Flicking slowly through the page of notes he'd made as Bruce described the plan, he committed the details to memory...

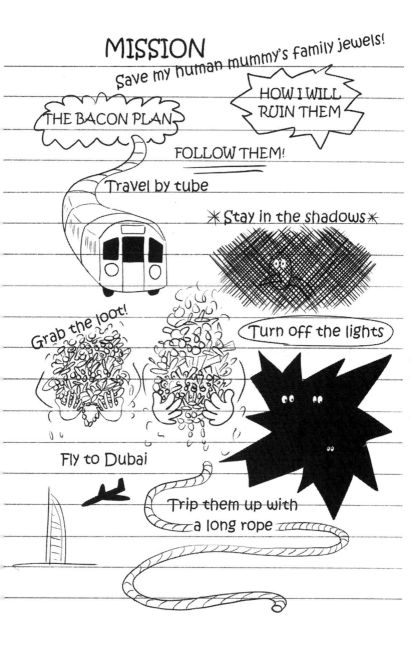

Now where on earth do I get a rope from? pondered Gus, flying around Putney Bridge looking for some. There was none in sight; it wasn't the kind of thing that humans carried around with them. Was there something else he could use…?

AHA! Scarves! Those stylish, light, pretty ones that humans wore in the summer! Oooh – that one would do…

Gus swooped down and filched a light blue silk neckerchief from a suave elderly gentleman walking along the river with his lady wife. 'GET OFF ME, YOU THIEVING GOOSE!' the man screeched. 'GIVE IT BACK – THAT'S A PRESENT FROM MY DAUGHTER…'

Unravelling it, Gus sighed, knowing immediately that it was too short to pull across the jewellery shop door. Harumph. Whilst trying to solve the problem, he tied it around his neck and admired his reflection in the river. *What a unique sense of style I have*, he told himself, thinking he couldn't wait to become human and go clothes-shopping at those big, exciting glass-walled shopping malls…

AHA! THAT WAS IT! He and the gentleman weren't the only ones to like clothes-shopping for stylish scarves! There were plenty more where this one came from – he could tie them all into one big, long colourful rope! Swooping down to find some more, he was so excited he flew into two feathery lumps, whipping up a cyclone wind of frenzied feathers… THOMASINA AND CUTHBERT!

'See, I told you he'd gone stark raving mad!' Gus heard Thomasina hiss to Cuthbert as they rearranged themselves mid-air and resumed holding wings. 'Just LOOK at him with that strange piece of material around his neck. *And* he was so rude to me when I bumped into him on my first of, what I hope to be, many modelling jobs! Whatever *next*?!'

Yes! Gus balled up his wing and fist-pumped the sky. Thomasina was dating Cuthbert! She was no longer in love with him; maybe his lack of enthusiasm for being painted whilst kissing her in the school art class was one snub too many! Yes, yes, triple yes!

Oh, this day was getting better and better!

'Oh, er, hi, Thomasina!' Gus smiled, waving his wing good-naturedly, before unsubtly letting out a massive sigh of relief. She fixed him with a beady-eyed glare.

Next, he laid out his scarves in a long row, admiring the diversity of designs. One was white with red and pink roses all over; there was even a royal-blue one with a white goose print all over it! Looping his beak in and out of the material, he tied each one to the end of the next, creating a super-colourful scarf rope.

As the sun set beautifully over the river – hey presto – he completed the final knot. It was now nearing bedtime and he felt an enormous sense of wellbeing. Tomorrow he would thwart the Bacon burglary, just as Grandad had stopped them at Cherry Blossom Farm. And EVEN better – he would save his Human Mummy's precious family jewels. Gus smiled. He almost felt sorry for Bruce and Spike – about to be thwarted by a goose *yet again*.

Then… it would all be over, and he could ask Grandad to arrange his meeting with Mr Goosman. With a wide smile on his beak, Gus fell asleep dreaming happy human dreams – in as little as half a week, he would be one for real!

THIRTY-NINE

THE BACONS PREPARE FOR THE BIG DAY

The following Monday evening, Bruce Bacon was like a kid at Christmas as he walked through the flat door, rubbing his fat hands greedily together. 'Ahh – that was a good 'un,' he said. 'Plenty of rich bankers on the way home from after-work beers with their mates… So many arrogant twerps with their fifty-pound notes held together by their fancy gold money clips – they won't miss them if old Brucey decided to pick-pocket a few! Now we can relax, Spikey! Enjoy our hard-earned pick-pocketings living the high life in Dubai, until I get on with the next task of fencing the stolen jewels!'

'Alright, Bruv!' chirped Spike from the lounge. 'Whadda ya say? Me didn't quite catch it!'

Bruce's face darkened as he saw Spike dressed from head to toe in his burglar gear, knitted balaclava included. He was holding an axe at the wrong end and swinging it from side to side.

'WHAT ON EARTH ARE YOU DOING?' shrieked Bruce.

'Just getting in some practise for tomorrow, innit, Bruv. Although it's a bit 'ard with that loud 'onking sound coming from the riverside. Me reckons there was some right angry goose down there with *that* din goin on!'

Bruce's face turned puce with rage. Tonight, *of all nights*, before the day they were to pull off a successful heist, the last thing he wanted to hear was anything to do with a flipping goose!

'We can't get the tube to Hatton Garden tomorrow dressed like burglars! We might as well hold up a sign saying "Lock Us Up and Throw Away the Key"! We must go in our smart-casual clothes, looking like two respectable men travelling into central London to buy jewellery for my girlfriend! THEN, we change into the burglar clothes in the alleyway, before changing back to make our getaway once the job is done! Get that stupid gear off NOW!'

'Alright, Bruv, keep ya hair on!' said Spike, pulling down his black burglar trousers revealing skinny, bony legs.

'Eurghhh, not in here! Are you *TRYING* to make me puke up my guts until there is nothing left in my poor, starved stomach?' screeched Bruce whilst simultaneously making retching noises. 'And why *on earth* are you holding the axe that way? You'll *never* be able to smash through that thick protective glass that jewellers use in their displays like *that*.'

'I fought it was the handle!' replied Spike, looking very confused.

'No, that's the business end of the axe, you *imbecile*! In fact, don't bother with the axe at all; leave all the smashing to me. Your puny, weedy arms won't manage it anyway!'

'Oh,' said Spike, looking rather crestfallen. Why did Bruce always have to be so mean to him? He only ever tried his best!

Bruce Bacon paced up and down. His skin was feeling itchy and his toes were tingling. Tomorrow was the day – the climax of all his hard work and planning. The day he would shake off the shame of being beaten by a goose last time round. The day he would resume his position as a respected member of the criminal underworld! And the day he would become richer than his wildest dreams!

'Go to your bedroom and put on your favourite teddy-bear PJs, Spike,' he said. 'We both need a good night's sleep before tomorrow!'

FORTY

I'LL TAKE YOU DOWN TO CHINATOWN

At 1.15pm, Gus boarded the tube at Putney Bridge with Bruce and Spike, both dressed smartly and each carrying a bag. He kept well back and close to the floor, his roll of scarves and pashminas tucked under his wing. He disembarked at Chancery Lane before discreetly following them down the alleyway nearest to Tom's jewellery shop.

The alley stank of rubbish from overflowing bins, with fat, juicy dead rats dotted here and there. In the corner of his eye, Gus noticed a pair of dangerous bright green eyes sizing him up from behind a bin.

'EatSSS mySSS dinner and I'll pluckSSS *every feather* from your miserable deadSSS body,' hissed a scraggy ginger alley cat, revealing itself from the shadows.

'You dare out-hiss a goose, Kitty, and I'll take ya down to Chinatown!' Gus replied, waving his balled-up wing like a fist.

'Hissssssssssssss,' replied the cat, sharpening its claws into daggers, ready to shred Gus to pieces.

'Arghhhhh,' Gus wailed, his bravado instantaneously evaporating. Hastily, he waddled behind the bins and jumped into the smallest one to hide.

'Not so hard now, are you, Goosey?' he heard the skanky fur-ball hiss, as it stalked around poking its nose and whiskers into discarded bits of rubbish trying to find him.

As luck would have it, Bruce and Spike were too busy changing into their burglar gear to have noticed the kerfuffle. Sinking into the old newspapers, food containers and sloppy bits of discarded food, Gus relaxed and prayed that there was no tikka masala sauce in this bin.

'Hey, look at me, Bruv, I am one of 'em majorette dancers like we seen on TV that one time!' Spike said from somewhere in front of his bin. Peeking up to get an eyeful, he saw Spike, now dressed in burglar gear, holding the axe at the wrong end and twirling it around as if he were a dancer with a twirling baton.

It was a *dreadful* sight. He looked like a stringy piece of spaghetti swirling in a pan. The axe handle span out of control and... WHACK! Bruce fell to the ground.

'Bruv, BRUV! Is you alive?' Spike yelped in panic. 'Don't drop dead on me! I can't do this 'ere heist without your big fat brain!'

He put his ear to Bruce's mouth and breathed a sigh of relief as a gush of smelly sausage breath came out. 'Ah, fank god for that! You is alive! Wake up now! Ah – I knows what! I fink you'll like this very much!'

Gus watched as Spike rustled around in his backpack and produced a thick black pen. Lifting the balaclava up from Bruce's unconscious head, he looked deep in concentration as he wrote something on Bruce's forehead:

BRUCE THE NUMBA 1 JOOLERY THIEF!

'There!' said Spike to himself. 'I knows you'd want everyone to know you's the best!' He then gently replaced the balaclava over his face.

All of a sudden, Gus felt a hot fur-ball land on his head.

'AH-HA! Found you now, Goosey! Prepare to DIE!'

Thinking quick and taking his inspiration from Spike, Gus turned his head sharply in the small space available and knocked out that stupid kitty with his beak. Now it was taking up too much space in the bin and suffocating him with its rotting fur. *For flip's sake, Bruce*, he thought to himself, *hurry up and regain consciousness so we can all get the hell out of here...*

'Woah, what happened?' he heard Bruce ask, stirring groggily.

'You started to look really pale and then fainted. Maybe one of 'em sausages you pigged for breakfast was off?' Spike lied.

Bruce got up quickly, wobbling a bit. He looked

at his watch. 'Drat! We MUST get on with this robbery NOW. Or we'll miss our flights to Dubai…

'Remember Spike, when we go in, *I* will do the talking as I sound more menacing! And *I* will do the smashing as I am bigger and better. Then *I* will swipe the jewellery as I am quicker and smarter, so know which pieces to grab in the limited time we have! All *you* need to do is stand at the door and alert me if you see anyone trying to come in and stop us! Just ONE small, insignificant job.

'Think you can handle that, dimwit?'

FORTY-ONE

JEWELLERY HEIST

'EVERYBODY STOP WHAT YOU ARE DOING AND PUT YOUR HANDS BEHIND YOUR HEAD!' screamed Bruce at the top of his fat, loud voice. Spike nervously tiptoed behind him, gripping on to the sides of Bruce's black jumper like he was cuddling his favourite teddy.

'ARGHHHHHHHH,' came a bloodcurdling screech of terror, out of the lipstick-smeared mouth of a human shop lady with bright blue eyeshadow.

'We're bein' robbed by a big fat thief and 'is accomplice! Quick, do wot 'e says, Clara!' she screeched at the little girl besides her.

Clara? What on earth was she doing in the shop today?!

'Awesome!' replied Clara. 'I was, like, so sad when Daddy said I must spend my school holidays helping in the shop, but this is, like… AWESOME!

205

For real life, a robbery! Just wait 'til I tell my school friends…'

'Arghhhhh! Clara, look over there – what's that? It looks like a goose pulling a coloured rope across the front door. Arghhhhhhhhhh… did you spike my afternoon coffee…'

'Oh, my golly gosh! I know THAT goose,' Clara shrieked, as Bruce Bacon yanked an axe out of his bag and began waving it wildly. He advanced menacingly in the direction of Babs the shop lady.

'Clara, get back from the counters, quick,' Babs screamed, droplets of sweat pouring down her face. 'I think he's gonna smash everything.'

They crouched down at the back of the shop, holding each other close, Clara's sweet little rosy cheeks switching to a ghostly white. The silver axe blade glittered under the shop lights. Their faces turned white, and they closed their eyes, as Bruce raised the axe above his head.

'DO IT, BRUV,' shouted Spike from his position behind Bruce. Spike covered his eyes with his hands. Suddenly Bruce brought the blade slamming down.

CRASH!

The middle counter smashed into pieces. Splinters of glass rose into the air and showered back down like rain. Bruce took a step to his right, raised the axe again and brought it down on the next glass counter.

CRASH!

Two big steps to the left, and he did the same again on the third and last glass counter.

CRASH!

Bruce had pieces of glass stuck in his hair like sharp snowflakes. But he didn't care.

'We did it, Spikey!' he shouted in triumph. 'Bring the bags over.' Before him lay three counters of sparkling jewellery, opened up and ready for him and Spike to steal. He greedily thrust his pudgy hand into the first one like a kid with a sweet jar.

At that precise moment a clear cloud of smelly fog blasted out from overhead, in the direction of Bruce and Spike.

First, it came out as an unpleasant, yet mild aroma…

'Babs – what's going on? Eww, gross! Have you just farted? I'm used to stinky smells, but that's even grosser than the boys at school!'

'Certainly not Clara! That's DISGUSTING! I've never smelled a fart so awful in my life. It reeks of fried sausages.' Now Babs was struggling to get the words out and her face had turned green.

Gus, enjoying have no sense of smell, heard her go 'Bleugh…bleugh…bleurghhhhhhhhh' as she threw up three fondant fancies and a cup of coffee all over the floor.

Clara's face registered confusion, then shock, then realisation as her whole life appeared to flash before her eyes…

'Arghh, I remember now… it's all coming back to me… that's *THE* goose. He was trying to tell me something all along! He's the ONE who hatched in my hands when I was eight and a quarter. Not just some annoying bird that's been stalking me! Babs – it all makes sense now! He's our FRIEND!

'We need help before this gets worse. I know – that goose will help!' Clara shrieked. She skidded across the slippery floor coated with Babs's sick, past Bruce, past Spike, and towards the door. Gus smiled and winked at Clara as she approached. He pointed his wing under the rope, indicating that Clara was small enough to sail right under it and out of the shop into daylight.

Lifting his wing, Gus turned out the shop lights and plunged the place into darkness, honking as if his life depended on it, just like Grandad did at the farm, many years ago.

'Quick, RUN! NOW!' Bruce screamed.

'But I can't see where I is going, Bruv! And that noisy goose honking is scaring me! You PROMISED there wouldn't be GOOSES this time! You is a big, fat liar, Bruv! I'm done with ya!'

Bruce ran towards the shop door with his bags of jewels, aiming for his big exit. Instead, he ran straight into Gus's makeshift rope pulled tight across the doorframe. He pinged off it like a ball from a slingshot, howling as he boomeranged straight back into the shop, knocking Spike out and landing on a chunky pile of Babs's sick.

'Over here, in here,' yelled Clara, running back into the shop with a group of security guards and a man with a camera. As the carnage began to end and the smell died down, Gus turned the shop-floor lights back on.

'This is him!' Clara exclaimed proudly. 'This is the hero goose that stopped my daddy's shop from being burgled!' She picked Gus up excitedly, twirling him around and planting a big kiss on his beak. It felt nice, like a hug from a dear friend. But he didn't feel that same rush of love and comfort as when Goosabella hugged him, the mummy who'd brought him up, been there for him since day one…

As Gus finished pondering who in fact his 'real mummy' was, one of the humans shoved a camera lens right in his face. 'SAY CHEESE FOR THE CAMERA, GOOSEY!'

FORTY-TWO

TWICE RUINED BY A GOOSE

The next morning Goosabella was out for her morning exercise. Mid-flight, she was flabbergasted to see a photograph of her son on the front page of the *River Mail* newspaper. She read the headline with her sharp eyesight and admired Gus's photo. Then, swooping down, she swiped a copy with her beak as the humans scattered off in different directions.

ARGHH GOOSE! ARGHH IT WANTS TO READ THE NEWS! ARGH IT'S GONNA GO FOR MY SALT AND VINEGAR CRISPS! AHH-AHH-ARGHGHHHHHHHHHHHHHH!

Quickly, she escaped from the ridiculous commotion, before flying to a quiet spot to read the news in peace.

The River Mail News

The two brothers, real names Willis Bacon and Shirley Bacon, attempted to steal thousands of pounds' worth of rare jewels from the Tom Stecker Jewellery Shop in Hatton Garden yesterday afternoon. These men, who go by their more widely known aliases, 'Bruce' and 'Spike', have been known to the police for over two decades, beginning their criminal careers as petty local thieves and gaining national recognition fifteen years ago, when an attempt to steal the engagement ring of a farmer's daughter was thwarted by a Guard Goose.

Ruined Reputation

After spending time in prison for the Cherry Blossom Farm robbery attempt, it appears that the reputation of Bruce Bacon in particular took a severe battering. Previously well known in the criminal world, working for the infamous original gangster 'Mad Dog O' Banion', Bruce emerged from HMP Wormwood Scrubs with no friends left. This was due to the nature of how the Cherry Blossom Farm robbery was thwarted. According to an old acquaintance who wishes to remain anonymous, no criminal would dare to be seen again in the company of a man who had been outwitted by a goose. Said the acquaintance, 'I know geese are meant to be hard as nails when compared to other animals, and they like to give it large with all that territorial hissing and honking, but at the end of the day, a goose is just an animal, which is below man in the pecking order, and about one fiftieth of the weight of Bruce Bacon. So no, I just couldn't associate with a man who has been outwitted by a farmyard animal.'

Twice Thwarted by a Goose

The esteemed former Prime Minister Sir Winston Churchill once said, 'All men make mistakes, but only wise men learn from mistakes.' It would seem that Bacon and Bacon learned nothing from how the thwarted Cherry Blossom Farm robbery ended, indicating that they are not wise men. Had they been smart, they would have realised that they are neither good at stealing jewellery nor outwitting Canada geese. Nonetheless, they proceeded to attempt a much more ambitious heist at the Tom Stecker Jewellery Shop. Barbara Moon, the 48-year-old shop assistant on duty when the heist happened, informed us, 'At first, I was absolutely terrified when this big, fat lout came in brandishing an axe, but the situation soon turned comical when the goose got involved. Even the Bobbies had a good old laugh when they got there. And when we heard that the criminals themselves manufactured the security system, Fart Fog, we laughed even more. I mean, what kind of idiot can't outsmart their own security system, let alone two geese! It gets better and better, you couldn't make this stuff up!'

See Page Seven for commentary, including 'Why Geese Would Make Great School Teachers', by Siegfried F. Goosman.

213

ETON SCHOLARSHIP FOR SON OF BRUCE BACON

Not all children born to criminals need to follow in their parents' footsteps, as demonstrated by Boris Bacon, the son of thwarted jewellery heist criminal, Bruce Bacon. At the tender age of 11, Boris not only has an exceptional I.Q. of 196, but has now won a 'New Foundation Scholarship' to  Eton College with full financial assistance. It appears that Junior Bacon, at least, is on track to exceed the intellect of even the most heroic riverside goose.

Due to start this September, Boris Bacon, when interviewed, told us, 'I am extremely proud to receive this great privilege, as I have an insatiable thirst for learning. I look forward to making the most of the many academic and extracurricular opportunities that such a fine school has to offer. I hope to become a High Court Judge when I am older and know that a first-rate education will help me achieve this, as I seek to distance myself from my family's criminal reputation.' The Headmaster of Eton is very much looking forward to welcoming Boris Bacon this September and commented, 'We wish to move Eton into the twenty first-century; we are no longer a school just for heirs to valuable jewels, but also sons of criminals who cannot even succeed in stealing valuable jewels.'

FORTY-THREE

IMPRINTING

Still sleepy from his adventure yesterday, Gus hauled himself out of his watery bed. He opened his notebook and flicked to the last page, smiling proudly at the big tick he'd drawn yesterday evening. Today was a very big day, the biggest – it was time to tick off that second goal. If all went to plan, tonight he would be resting his head on a goose-feather pillow and loafing under a soft duvet.

My Goals — by Gus

✓   Save my Human Mummy's family jewels from the evil Bacons

✗   Meet Mr Goosman so he can turn me into a human

Grandad's shadow loomed large. 'Come on, Gus, we'd better get going – we can't keep Mr Goosman waiting.'

'Coming, Grandad,' Gus replied, smoothing down his head feathers so he looked his absolute best. He waddled after Grandad and the two of them took off up into the sky. They flew over bright green fields and yellow rows of corn that seemed to go on forever.

'Come on, Gus, keep up! I'm a withered old goose and I'm managing to outfly you this morning. Whatever's wrong?' asked Grandad.

'Oh, just so many thoughts going through my head and I'm a bit nervous. Thinking this much is slowing me down – I'm not used to it!'

'In a few minutes we'll be there,' said Grandad, breaking Gus's deep thoughts. 'Don't be nervous. Siegfried's a lovely man and we've known each other for years, he'll be very understanding and do whatever he can to help.'

They flew on in silence until Grandad indicated with his flight feather that they were near their destination and must begin their descent. Swooping and flying to a standstill, they arrived at the front door of Mr Goosman's cottage. It was in the middle of a lovely, chocolate-box style English village.

Gus surveyed the stucco-fronted cottage with a thatched roof, enveloping it like melted cheese. There were flower boxes underneath the windows, with fuchsia peonies poking out proudly. The front door, which was painted sage green, had a brass door knocker at human shoulder height, and a smaller brass, goose-shaped door knocker lower down at wing height. Reaching out his wing, Grandad knocked it with a rat-a-tat-tat.

'Why, hello,' said Mr Goosman, as if talking to his dearest old friend. Gus admired his tweed suit, accessorised with a silk neck scarf secured by a gold brooch in the shape of a wild goose.

'I've been expecting you both! Your dear grandfather has told me so much about you, Gus,' he said, laughing melodically. 'Why, why, do come in. The tea's just brewing, and I have chocolate biscuits, your favourite,' he continued, smiling at Grandad.

'It's a pleasure to see you as always, Siegfried,' said Grandad.

'Pleased to, uh, meet you, Mr Goosman,' stuttered Gus.

'Oh no, you MUST call me Siegfried, I insist! I've *so* been looking forward to meeting you, Gus. Now, sit down,' he said, gesturing towards two comfy-looking goose-sized armchairs in front of a wooden table and opposite a large human-sized sofa.

'Before I serve you both tea and biscuits, tell me something important, Gus. Would you like your grandad to stay for support, or would you like to have a conversation in private before I catch up with him? I understand from what he tells me that you wish to know if I can help you achieve your deepest desire – becoming a human being. Sometimes when geese visit me for advice, they want to have a confidential chat.'

'I'm happy for him to stay,' said Gus. 'He knows everything about me and the way I feel about being a goose, anyway.'

'Alright, of course, if that's what you prefer,' said Mr Goosman, putting down a plate of chocolate biscuits and pouring three cups of tea. Within a few seconds, Grandad had inhaled five biscuits, but Gus felt too nervous to eat. Instead, he slowly sipped his tea with his beak, testing sentences in his mind – to see if they sounded intelligent – before saying them aloud.

'So, you mention the way you feel about being a goose,' Mr Goosman asked gently.

'Yes, I just hate being one. Everything about them is so *sooo boring*. There's nothing to aspire to. And Mum keeps pressuring me to be Prime Goose, which is utterly pointless! There's nothing to look forward to, no incentive to work hard, no, no, no, uh… nothing,' he stammered, tears welling up like when he had this same chat with Grandad.

'And yes,' Gus continued, 'I might enjoy having a family, a goose wife, some goslings and all that, everything a *normal* goose wants when they grow up. But again, for what? It's not as if my future wife will have anything interesting to say, anyway.

All lady geese are dull and just spend time sipping river water whilst gossiping about each other and preening their feathers! After all, she'd just be a goose, so I can hardly expect anything more!'

Mr Goosman looked thoughtful, chewing on the end of his fountain pen in between taking notes.

Gently putting his hand on Gus's wing, he asked, 'So what is it you would like me to do to help?'

Gus sat quietly for a few minutes, sniffling through tears. Mr Goosman held out a box of tissues. Gratefully he took one with his wing and noisily blew his beak.

'Well, I was hoping you could transform me into a human being.' There, he had said it.

'Why is it that you want to become human?'

'There are so many reasons it's hard to know where to start,' replied Gus.

'Why don't you begin by telling me where these feelings first came from?'

'It actually began the very moment I was born! My mum told me this story about how my egg rolled into a children's playground and a little girl picked it up. Before she had a chance to give the egg back to Mum, I hatched in the human girl's hands. I always knew that I was different and didn't really fit in, but after I heard this story, I suddenly understood why. The feeling kind of grew from there, I guess. The more I saw of humans, the more I wanted to be one. They have more varied, exciting lives. I don't want to float in a dirty river and eat grass – I want to eat a cheeseburger at McDonald's and then stay up all night on my PlayStation…

'And then Grandad told me all about his awesome adventures on Cherry Blossom Farm! It was the final push that I needed to pursue my dream of becoming human, and have a much more exciting life than I can ever have as a DULL OLD GOOSE!' Gus practically shouted the last words as he got more and more excited that someone who could actually do something about his problem was finally listening.

Mr Goosman put his hand gently on Gus's wing and smiled. 'Did you know, Gus, that what happened to you actually has a name? It's called "imprinting". Geese don't actually know that they're geese when they first hatch, so the first thing they see is what they think they are. This is why you identify so closely with humans.'

Gus glanced up at Mr Goosman and saw sympathy and understanding in his piercing eyes. He held his breath. This was the biggest moment of his biggest day. He felt closer than ever before to becoming a human instead of a goose. Mr Goosman was on the verge of telling him that he would transform him into what he was always meant to be: human. He could feel it in his feathers…

FORTY-FOUR

GIVE GEESE A CHANCE

'Right, Gus, here goes,' said Mr Goosman, fixing him with his sharp eyes. 'The first thing you need to know, and I wish I wasn't the one having to tell you this, is that I'm not able to transform you into a human being. Not just me, no one can. No such technology that would allow this to happen exists. And it is unlikely it ever will. Yes, we can play games – virtual reality, they call it – where humans can pretend to be geese, and I am sure it is not beyond the wit of man to invent ones where geese can imagine they are human. But the true reality of this is it's just not possible. The laws of the universe and nature won't allow it. I hate to disappoint you, Gus, but I cannot give you false hope. You will never become human. I'm so sorry.'

Gus stared at Mr Goosman in shock. What was he hearing?

Noooooo!

He refused to believe it. He so much wanted to become human, and if he wished it strongly enough, it could still happen, couldn't it? He opened his beak to speak, but no words came out. He hung his head and staggered backwards. Grandad rushed across to catch him.

'I'm so sorry, Gus,' he said, wrapping his wings around his grandson. 'I know this is the last thing you wanted to hear.'

Mr Goosman was still speaking. Gus tried to focus.

'But this doesn't have to be the end of your hopes and dreams, Gus. There are other ways for you, as a goose, to achieve happiness and fulfilment, and, I believe, over time you will come to understand this and go on to live a great life.'

Gus's mind was spinning. His legs wobbled.

'You know, Gus,' continued Mr Goosman, 'in this world, whether you are a human, goose, fox or even something else entirely, there are things you can change and things that you can't. It helps to begin by identifying what makes you unhappy, which you have already done. Then, change the things you *can*, and make the most of the ones that you *can't*. You know, the grass is not always greener, anyway. Even if I had been able to transform you into a human, you would be swapping one set of problems for another.'

Gus sank back into Grandad's soft feathers. Tears dripped from his eyes. He didn't even try to wipe them away.

'To address your situation specifically, though, if you can't change the status quo – that is, being a goose – maybe you should think about changing your environment. Have a think about all those things that you love about the human world. Can some of these be copied in the goose community for *all geese* to enjoy?'

Mr Goosman was gazing at Gus with big, kind eyes.

'And another thing... I think you should give your own species a chance. Not all geese are dull, hissy lumps of feathers. You should never judge a book by its cover. Why don't you give geese a chance? Get to know them better, speak to them more. I've have had many a fascinating conversation with a goose! And if after giving your current friends a good chance you still find them dull, maybe you should mingle more with the wider flock, get to know some new lady geese and ganders, who might be more your kind of goose?'

'But what about my real Human Mummy? The special human whose hands I hatched into. I think about her all the time.'

'Remember, Gus, that a mother is not the first person you see but the person who has loved and cared for you your whole life... the one who helped you scavenge your first breakfast, take your first flight… Goosabella is your *real* mummy, she's the one who loves you unconditionally. Give her more of a chance too,' Mr Goosman replied wisely.

'I say again, Gus, I'm so sorry to disappoint you. But before we say our goodbyes, I want to leave you with this. My favourite quote is one by a human philosopher called Immanuel Kant. Kant said that the rules of happiness are "Something to do, someone to love, something to hope for". Think about how these things can be achieved by a smart, mature, young gander, just like you.'

Mr Goosman took off his red silk scarf, placed it around Gus's neck and fastened it with the gold goose brooch. 'I want you to keep this,' he said. 'The silk scarf is so you understand that a goose can enjoy things from the human world; the brooch is to remind you that your own species is a truly beautiful thing.'

*

Grandad helped Gus make it home. Gus felt a huge emptiness in his heart. He hardly had the strength to fly, and he crash-landed on water and muddy banks many times. Every time, Grandad helped him up. When he finally made it home, he saw Mum waving a newspaper page with a photo of him on it!

'Gus, Gus! I can't believe this is you and that YOU alone managed this! It's hard enough outwitting animal predators, but this is a whole other level of achievement! Stopping not one but TWO human thieves. And in such a clever, well-thought-out way! I had no idea that you could even tie knots! I'm so proud of you I'm going to cry.'

Gus felt Mum's warm tears roll down his feathers as she embraced him with her wide, protective wings. Soon he felt tears start to run down his beak again, too. He was crying not just because his dream was over but because he loved Mum so very much. He would never become human, but remaining a goose would not part them.

FORTY-FIVE

THE BEST OF EVERYTHING

One Month Later: Selection Panel for Prime Goose Finalists

Gus had just finished delivering his ten-minute speech on 'What Being Prime Goose Would Mean to Him'. It was a nerve-racking experience, and the selection panel, which Dad had chosen, asked some very difficult questions. But Gus was proud of his performance. He felt that he held his own and came across as a very mature gander, looking the part in his red neck scarf and goose brooch.

It had been the wise words of Mr Siegfried F. Goosman that made him run for Prime Goose in the end. Mr Goosman was right. If he couldn't become human, there was nothing to stop him making changes in the goose community and copying bits of the human world that he loved most. Gus decided that ultimately, the easiest way to do this was to become Prime Goose, thereby winning the power to effectively make change. And, if he didn't get elected Prime Goose, then that didn't matter either. He'd learnt he was quite resilient to setbacks and that there was often another route to happiness when things didn't work out as planned. You just had to find another way.

After delivering his speech, he floated leisurely in the sun a few metres from where the Prime Goose Semi-Final was taking place. A young lady goose swam towards him. He didn't know her but recognised her as the lady goose that had queued up behind him, waiting to deliver her speech for the panel.

'Hi, I'm Lucinda,' she honked, confidently stretching out a slender wing to greet him.

Gus smiled at her. Taking in her unfamiliar features with his shiny black eyes, he noticed immediately that she had lovely, tidy feathers, an elegant neck and sparkling eyes. She wasn't preened and pampered in the obvious way that Thomasina and her friends were; her look was more natural. Something Gus liked. And those eyes – they were so sparkly and enigmatic!

'I recognise you vaguely from being in the same flock. You hang out with Cuthbert, Thomasina and crew, don't you?'

'Guilty as charged,' joked Gus. 'But actually, I'm trying to make more of an effort to meet other geese in the flock lately, instead of just sticking to the same crew. So, it's a real pleasure to meet you! How did your speech go?'

'Oh, I'm pretty sure it went well. I'm smart, and I worked very hard on it,' she replied, as if simply stating facts and without the faintest hint of arrogance. 'But you never know, do you? There were a few lady geese on the panel, but I guess it depends on whether my style of Feathered Feminism goes down well. I know it isn't for everyone!' She gave a bright little laugh that made her eyes twinkle even more.

'Feathered Feminism?' asked Gus, intrigued.

'Yes,' said Lucinda. 'Though this flock has come very far in terms of making everyone feel welcome, I feel more could be done to give equal rights to lady geese. Although admittedly I *would* like some goslings myself one day, I happen to have more to me than that! I want to make a real difference to the lives of geese in our community, and to be the flock leader, hopefully inspiring the next generation of young, female goslings.'

'Oh,' said Gus, 'I see your point. My mum, Goosabella, is one of the smartest, bravest geese ever. In fact, I think it's really her that runs the flock with my father saying what she tells him to.'

They both honked with laughter, enjoying relaxing in the sun.

'So, tell me, what would *you* do, if you are elected Prime Goose?' Lucinda asked, eyes twinkling.

'Ah, it's a long story, but I think there are other species and communities beyond our own that have a better way of doing things. In some but not all aspects, I must add. For example, in the human community, the harder you work, the nicer the things you can buy. Hard work seems to allow them to buy nicer homes and enjoy doing more exciting things, such as going to restaurants for tasty food! So, there's an incentive to work towards something. Their life is more varied too: there are lots of different jobs you could do, lots of fun clothes to wear; the list goes on. That variety must be very stimulating. I think some of those ideas could work well for geese. If I am chosen as a Prime Goose finalist, my slogan will be "Best of Everything", meaning we should steal the best bits of other communities for our own.'

Gus gazed at Lucinda. It was a strange feeling to have a female goose of his age apparently genuinely interested in what he was saying.

'I did a lot of research already, actually, spying on humans for ideas. I've had some fantastic adventures. I'll tell you more about it one day, if you'd like?'

'Wow, you spy on humans? Me too! You know The Grand Goose Hotel? I love people-watching there. It's very inspirational seeing all those high-powered female human beings with successful careers, enjoying business lunches there. You know, I didn't think any other goose besides me was as interested in the world outside our own as I am...'

As Lucinda carried on honking, Gus found himself completely absorbed in what she had to say. Maybe geese weren't so dull, and maybe it wasn't so bad being one after all…

EPILOGUE

A FEW DAYS LATER, DUB-WOTSIT (A.K.A. DUBAI)

''Ere, pass me the suntan lotion, please, my darlin' ickle Treacle Tart,' Spike Bacon said to the woman looking lovingly at him. They were lounging on sunbeds side by side on Jumeirah Beach in Dubai.

'Here you go, my cutie ickle Snuggle-Bums,' she cooed back.

'Ah, now dis is the LIFE!' said Spike, rubbing his bony limbs and pigeon chest with lotion. He smiled happily to himself as he thought of the romantic supper planned for that evening, when he was going to pop THE question. It was rather soon in the relationship to ask her to marry him, but he was confident she would say yes.

Spike was a new, more confident and all round better human being these days. In fact, he felt as if his life was just beginning and he was very thankful to that clever Canada goose for sending him in a happier direction. Counting his blessings, he leaned over and tenderly kissed his girlfriend, Ciggy Cheryl, on the forehead. He liked to call her 'Treacle Tart', which he heard when watching *EastEnders* one day and understood to be cockney rhyming slang for 'sweetheart'.

'How's about a tasty, fruity cocktail, darlin' Treacle?'

'Oooh, well, don't mind if I do! Delish!' replied Cheryl, smiling so widely she displayed *every single one* of her yellow, tobacco-stained teeth.

'Oh, while I remember, after we 'ave drunk our cocktails, will ya help me write a good-luck card to send to me nephew, Boris? I want 'im to know I is thinking of him when 'e 'as 'is first day at that posho school! I need 'elp wiv spelling some words, though. Boris is dead clever and 'e will know if his silly uncle gets it wrong!'

'Of course I will, darlin' Spikey. You're *so* thoughtful and kind. Anything for you, Snuggle-Bums,' replied Cheryl.

They stood up and walked hand in hand to the cocktail bar on the beach, just in front of the Burj Al Arab, a very fancy hotel in Dubai where they were staying.

Things had worked out rather well for Spike Bacon. It was probably about time he was due some luck, anyway. After the police questioned him about the attempted jewellery heist, they concluded he was merely an innocent tag-along, too stupid to understand that what he'd done was wrong. They decided Bruce was the *real* criminal mastermind and threw him into jail for three years. Spike, on the other hand, had been released due to being too stupid to be culpable. And Spike sure wasn't going to argue with that decision!

That fateful day, he'd sauntered out of the police station, but not before hugging his 'dear' brother goodbye and gently removing a huge wodge of cash from his pocket. It was the money Bruce had stolen from city bankers to keep himself going until he fenced the stolen jewels. Spike didn't feel bad, though. Although he was extremely dim, he knew Bruce would have done exactly the same thing!

As luck would have it, on emerging from the police station, Spike bumped into his ex, and only ever, girlfriend, Ciggy Cheryl. Ciggy Cheryl was just having a cigarette outside the police station before heading home. She had been hauled into the station handcuffed when she forgot to pay for a pack of fags at a nearby supermarket. After questioning her, the police realised that it was a genuine mistake, she had simply forgotten, and was in fact a ditzy but dear-hearted soul as opposed to a naughty shop thief. Therefore, like Spike, she'd been released.

Recognising each other, the pair instantly hit it off again. Spike loved spending time with her. She was a kind, good-hearted person who brought out the best in him. And she was much nicer to him than Bruce ever was. They should never have split up in their youth and he vowed never to let go of her again. So, falling madly in love, the two of them decided to take a romantic holiday to that place that Spike called 'Dub-wotsit'. Using Bruce's cash.

'Ooooh, look, Chezza! GOOSES!' Spike shrieked

happily as he saw a migratory flock in the sky beginning their descent.

*

The South West London Flock of Geese, led by Gus Senior, Gus's Dad, landed on the sandy shores of Dubai. They made quite an entrance with all their noisy hissing, honking and flapping. This would be Gus Senior's last flight leading the geese as they flew in their usual V-shape. At the end of their trip, the new Prime Goose would be announced.

After an emotional few weeks, Gus had asked his dad if he would invite the whole flock to take a holiday in Dubai. Feeling exceptionally proud of his son and his recent achievements, including both thwarting the jewellery heist and being selected as one of two finalists in the Prime Goose election process, Gus Senior was only too happy to oblige.

Gus himself fancied a holiday after all his hard work and was quite intrigued by Dubai after hearing Bruce and Spike discuss it. He was also excited to explore it with Lucinda, the other Prime Goose finalist, who he had just started dating. They looked forward to some human-watching together, as well as trying the different types of Middle Eastern cuisine that she and Gus could swipe off the plates of native and holiday-making humans.

*

To this day, Gus may still be a goose, but he is a genuinely happy one: having found something to do, something to hope for and someone to love. In fact, there were many to love: Grandad, Mum, Dad and now his new goose wife that he was so proud of, the first ever Lady Prime Goose, Lucinda.

ABOUT THE AUTHOR

After giving birth to my daughter Clara, I spent her nap times achieving a life ambition: writing my debut novel. Gus the Canada goose is a natural central character: I saw him, his family and friends flying and swimming outside the London flat where I once lived. I also heard their loud hisses and honks, which often interrupted me as I wrote about their vibrant goose community. This, combined with my career as a digital business consultant, inspired the idea for my novel. As humans our lives are exciting and varied: I enjoy reading great books, shopping for vintage fashion, eating delicious food and am lucky enough to have an interesting career where I can try a VR headset for fun. Geese have none of these things; they may indeed want it all too…

ACKNOWLEDGEMENTS

I would like to thank everyone who helped and supported me in writing my debut novel.

My greatest thanks to Gary Johnson, the wonderful and extremely talented artist who helped bring my story to life. I would also like to thank Ian Johnson, my Critique Partner, who was instrumental in refining earlier versions. Also, to Antonia Prescott from Cornerstones Literary Consultancy, who taught me so much and has given me the skills and confidence to write more. All three were a joy to work with and without them I would not be ready to publish today.

I would also like to thank my various beta readers who kindly took the time to read and advise on early drafts – thank you so much to Alexis Faulkner, Helen Wellington, Paul Francis, Dawn and Simon Coleman (my amazing parents who I love very much and have supported me in everything I have ever done – I could not have chosen better parents in life!). Thank you to my husband Philip, for proof-reading, spotting and fixing continuity errors, and intellectual property guidance.

My most important test readers are without a doubt the children from the age range at which the novel is aimed. Thank you to all the pupils at St Martin's School in Solihull who read an earlier version of the novel and completed feedback forms. A particular thank-you also to Ariana Kaur, a lovely girl who gave me some great ideas to incorporate during an enjoyable Zoom call.

Finally, thank you to Clara and Alexander, my children. I love you both very much and wrote this for you. Clara, you gave me some wonderful ideas and I love the artwork you created for Chapter 20.

Alexander, I'll steal your ideas for my next novel!